GAJINDER OBEROI

stories

that remain untold

GAJINDER OBEROI

stories

that remain untold

40

Publisher: Forty South Publishing
www.fortysouth.com.au

Printer: IngramSpark

Cover Illustration: Agnieszka Sikorska-Meikle

Design & Typeset: Imogen Brown

contents

Foreword 7

Introduction 9

A Fallen Hero 11

The Last Salute 29

Forgotten Sunrise 43

Vanishing Frontiers 49

Death of a Tree God 53

My Home is in the Stars 59

Living in Afterlife 71

An Angel Warrior 75

Mirroring a Smile 83

Ravana's Third Rib 87

The Feast 101

foreword

The world of writing is such that people meet over time and space through the stories they write and share with each other and the rest of humanity. In today's day, humanity is a word that is not given the respect it deserves. But of all us practitioners of several professions, perhaps the medical profession is one that still believes in the term, and works under its conditions, to serve the rest of us.

So when a medical professional who has written several stories over a period of time brings them out of the bottom drawer of his desk, dusts them off and wants to send them out to the world to be read, it is certain that these stories will ring with the compassion, understanding and empathy. Even a degree of understandable pessimism, for his encounter with pain and death is as real as his encounter with other aspects of human behaviour.

Gajinder Oberoi is a pain management specialist, practising in Australia, and I am an author and editor, writing and teaching in India. It was Gajinder's stories that connected the two of us, since he asked if I would have a look at them and edit them for him. When we began working together, he was clear that he would send them one by one, and I had to edit them one by one, and though I found that different from the usual, I also considered it quite doable. There seemed to be no time constraint and this could also be because in these days of the pandemic, time had come to a standstill. According to Gajinder, it was the lockdown due to the pandemic that gave him the time to put together the scraps of writing he had done over the years and turn them into workable stories.

These stories are diverse, as diverse as the life experiences of the writer. A large part of any writer's success lies in his ability to look at the world from the protagonist's perspective, and convey this through his words to the reader, and allow the reader to connect with the protagonist's world, his thoughts and feelings. The lead story, titled 'A Fallen Hero', is heart-wrenching in its telling of how a small-town boy, failing to meet his father's wish that he become an engineer, gets disheartened, falls into the wrong company and then what follows is tragic. 'Death of a Tree God' shows the tenacity of a young boy and the cruelty of those with vested interests. 'My Home is in the Stars' is set in the turbulent time of Partition, and highlights how our experience in life impacts our own behaviour. Hatred begets hatred, and will emerge in the form of violence against those vulnerable and captive. 'An Afterlife' is an old man's attempt at building a spectacular life for himself after his death. Despite the darkness of the stories, some hold the promise of hope. 'Mirroring a Smile' is one such story.

The stories don't preach. Instead, they show us life's truths and how we try to come to terms with them as best we can.

Abha Iyengar,

New Delhi, 12 June 2020

Abha Iyengar is an internationally published, award-winning poet, author, editor and a British Council certified Creative Writing Mentor. Her work has appeared in several literary magazines and journals. She has six published books to her credit.

Introduction

Over last few decades, whenever an idea or a memory flashed across my mind, I would scribble it on a piece of paper and hoard it away. Unnoticed, the hidden collection continued to grow over the years. It may have never seen the light of the day but for the forced lockdown under Corona. The time, which may have been difficult to pass otherwise, provided an opportunity to explore these hidden treasures.

Put into a shape with a fictional touch these scribbles started to take the shape of engrossing tales. Many were a poignant reminder of a grim past.

The ones from India portray the realities of life from that bygone era from the 1950s to 1970s, highlighting the social upheaval in India during the period of "making a nation". It was a cultural and economic revolution during which many dreams became a reality and many others came crashing down. During those times, even when struggling for mere existence, fierce ambitions burned in the hearts of so many. One such example is that of Vasu in my story "Ravana's Third Rib". Though my protagonist fights for his day-to-day survival, he never stops dreaming.

This collection is a humble attempt to preserve those historical facts of our lives for future generations while wondering how much of this, unfortunately, still exists in our society.

Not all tales are my personal observation or imagination. There are pieces which come from what I heard as a child and remained with me ever after. "My Home is in the Stars" is one such example about the 1947 calamity. Then there is merciless exploitation of gullible souls in "A Fallen Hero" and "Death of a Tree God".

The interior mental conflict in those who are exploited doesn't just stay with them during that chapter of life but persists even if they survive, as seen in "The Last Salute". Sadly, in most cases the outcome is defeat at the hands of the exploiters, often by deceit.

These conflicts are still rampant in our society though the cause or effect may have changed. There is, however, a respite. We do observe pantheistic or naturalistic streaks in our protagonists. Some examples are Tomas in "An Angel Warrior", Daman in "A Fallen Hero" and Vasu in "Ravana's Third Rib". Perhaps it was their emancipation strategy.

Challenging life struggles also create prosaic characters in our society, again a survival strategy or living in denial, as is shown by Daman's father in "A Fallen Hero". The presence of superstitions or spiritual qualities, as seen in both Daman's mother in "A Fallen Hero" and Tomas in "An Angel Warrior", are ways for people to cope with these travesties or conflicts in our society in a different way.

In the tales set in more modern times, the stories' moral frameworks adopt a different outlook. People remain naive and in thrall to their dreams, and innocents continue to be exploited. This is evident in "Living in Afterlife".

Every piece has been spun to focus on a particular aspect of a character's struggle during a single chapter of his life. This gives a narrow time-scale, just like opening a chapter in the big book of life. In some of my stories, this has turned out to be the last chapter.

Nothing is of preternatural occurrence, all of it results from heartless and barbaric acts. And while I must apologize for giving a sordid end to many a story, it is indeed the reality of life, particularly for the innocent ones.

Gajinder Oberoi
Hobart, Australia
July 2020

A Fallen Hero

It was an unusually warm and quiet April night. The strong winds that usually blew this time of the year were silent. Also absent were the whistling sounds they produced as they flowed through the thick vegetation surrounding the sleepy town of Barkhapur in northern India, on the banks of the Barkha river.

There was, however, a storm brewing in Daman's head. He had spent the night tossing and turning, troubled by fears of shattered childhood dreams. The intermittent naps he did manage were abruptly broken by panic attacks, drenching him in cold sweat. The ceiling fan rotating in leisurely fashion overhead also failed to provide any comfort.

His high school results, to be announced next day, would determine his eligibility to become an engineer. This was his – and more particularly his father's – long-cherished dream. They strongly believed this to be the only hope to improve their lot and catapult their family to higher social status. Failure would also mean Daman losing the opportunity of making himself suitable for marrying Rima, the daughter of his father's engineer boss, a desire deep in Daman's heart.

For years, his father had nurtured these desires. Whenever Daman's schoolwork seemed to be slipping, he had developed a habit of making sarcastic remarks. In an attempt to make his son work harder and to avoid the destruction of his dreams, he repeatedly accused Daman of incompetence. Daman had spent this sleepless night dreading the effect his failure to secure the required grade would have on his father as well as on his own future.

He had in the past endured the poisonous barbs of his father's words by withdrawing into his own imaginary world, revolving around Rima. His dream world helped him survive the harsh verbal barbs. Sadly, his relationship with Rima was limited to his imaginary world alone, since he could never muster enough courage to reveal his hidden passion to her. Yet he strongly believed that one day, circumstances would unite them.

*

Very few inhabitants of Barkhapur's hundred thousand population knew the meaning of "freedom of expression". Sadness was an integral part of their lives, with a majority of them either farm labourers or low-wage office workers. Many lived under the fear of prosecution by corrupt policemen and bureaucrats, or under constant threat of repression by the powerful sections of the society. Agricultural production – mainly sugarcane and seasonal vegetables – along with a few small-scale industrial facilities, were the mainstay of the local economy. The town had some poorly maintained roads and basic infrastructure.

Some government offices did exist to provide necessary community services. Daman's father was a clerk in one of these offices, which looked after the city's water supply system. Like many other inhabitants of Barkhapur, he had always lived in an atmosphere of insecurity about his future and maintained very few contacts with people outside his family. Lack of creative mental and physical engagements had predisposed his mind to invent unfounded fears. He went through cycles of depression and paranoia, which had a very demoralising effect on both his wife and son. The only salvation for him in his mind was the hope that one day his son would become an engineer and equal his boss's status.

Because of this, Daman remained on the receiving end of his ongoing sarcastic tirades; regular harsh reminders to make him work hard to accomplish his dreams. These repeated remarks had planted similar fears in Daman's mind, shrivelling his self-confidence. Over time, Daman had started to strongly believe that his life would be meaningless if he failed to become an engineer.

*

Loud sounds of chirping and ruffling of feathers from a group of parrots on a guava tree in their backyard announced the breaking daylight. It was a nice and bright morning, but this natural wake-up call was not at all soothing to Daman's ears – sounded more like an unpleasant alarm to him.

"Daman, go and have a wash and pay your obeisance to God before you eat anything. Today is your result day," reminded his mother in a voice as sweet and soft as always. She had somehow maintained her sanity and peace in this city of sorrows through her religious devotion.

"I just came back from the morning prayers in the temple with your father. We have brought some prasad for you. You must eat it, to gain God's blessings before you go. Your father has been very worried about your result and has left early for his office."

She spoke, standing at the door of his room, ensuring he got out of bed, but Daman did not respond to her words.

She had persistently maintained her pride and affection for him and remained certain of his success.

Daman, his spirit slightly soothed because his father was not around to remind him once more about his impending failure, hurried through his morning rituals. Then he walked out of his house without eating or seeking God's blessings. He had no appetite for food and no desire to make a last-minute attempt to appease the Almighty when his fate had already been written and sealed in the pages of an official gazette.

*

Daman was a seventeen-year-old boy, of short stature, on the threshold of manhood. Though his family atmosphere had inhibited his power of expression, his large expressive eyes spoke for him and attracted the attention of people around him. His reticent bearing, particularly his eyes, conveyed fear rather than the mischief expected from boys his age. He looked like an exploitable young man.

Today the fear in his eyes was even deeper than usual.

His walk towards school was slow and reluctant, shuffling steps a sign of conflicting directives from his brain about the direction to follow.

Once in the school compound he saw a big crowd gathered around a notice board displaying the lists of high school results. His vision started to blur as he stood, perhaps paralysed by fear. His legs felt weak as he stood there motionless, not making any attempt to advance through the crowd to read the list.

"What is your roll number?" A piercing voice shook him out of his state of dissociation. "Tell me your roll number, young man."

Daman looked up; it was Sanga, a tall boy with a dishevelled and stern look.

Sanga must have noticed his state of paralysis and despair. Daman recalled him as a senior student who had been expelled from the school a few years ago due to his unlawful activities. Thereafter, he had earned the reputation of being a political activist – even a suspected terrorist. He had recently been involved in an attack on a local police officer and jailed for a short term. Daman quickly scratched his roll number on a piece of paper from his pocket and gave it to him. Sanga proceeded promptly towards the notice board, shoving his way through the crowd. He was back soon with Daman's marks scribbled on the paper.

Daman stood with an expressionless face when Sanga handed the slip to him. Sanga patted him on his shoulder and said in a consoling tone, "Take it easy, I will catch up with you later. Come to see me if you need any help. I am sure you know me."

The interaction was all so sudden and unexpected that Daman could not even muster words of thanks. The slip, held loosely in his sweaty hand, bore a number which was going to determine the future course of his life's journey.

Daman retreated towards his favourite spot in a remote corner of his school grounds. This spot was under a big palash tree on the banks of the Barkha river, at the edge of a thick forest that spread towards the foothills of a small mountain range.

Once there, he slowly opened the moist and twisted slip and read the result recorded there. He threw back his head in desperation and crushed the bearer of his misfortune in his fist. The pallor in his face deepened and his eyes turned expressionless.

Daman looked up to see a few bright palash flowers, bravely staying alive in the face of an arriving summer. He quietly observed the intermittent fall of dried flowers and leaves. Their gentle, swaying motion made his sleep-deprived eyes heavy and he drifted into a deep sleep.

His sleep was initially a pleasant and blissful trance but he soon sank into a state of tribulation, and small beads of cold sweat slowly emerged on his broad forehead.

*

All of a sudden, he was woken up by a strong shake and a resonant voice, "Daman, what the hell are you doing here?" His father was standing before him. "I've spent hours searching for you, along with our neighbours."

Daman was startled by his father's presence and the darkness of the night.

His father addressed a man standing close to him among other accompanying strangers. His voice was heavy, broken with emotion and suppressed anger. "He has lost his sense, Palta Sahib, a venomous snake could have easily killed him here."

He said, now looking at Daman, "Your mother is dying with anxiety and here you are with no concern either for her, or for my honour in the neighbourhood."

Daman continued to wear a baffled look, amazed at having slept into the night and the sudden appearance of this group of people. He looked at his father and heaved a deep sigh, then quietly followed him home.

He walked past a bench in his school garden, where he had once shared his lunch with Rima. He walked past the palatial white house of rich Nuri Seth, on the city's main road. These two landmarks had always been associated with his childhood dreams of a life of prosperity and eternal love.

After criss-crossing a few small lanes, they reached the street where he lived. He could see his mother standing at the other end of the street outside their house. "Where were you, my son?" she spoke in an emotional tone, fighting back her tears.

"Do not make a scene in the street," said Daman's father, dragging him inside the house.

Daman looked at his mother and could not hold back his tears. He fell into her arms, and they walked towards his room.

"Daman, please eat something first," she pleaded, but he did not respond.

He spent the rest of the night lying in his bed and blankly staring at the ceiling fan's slow relentless cycles. He could hear the heated debate from the other room with his mother trying in vain to calm his father, who continued to blame Daman for his irresponsible attitude to life.

"Even when you are going for a short journey you make a detailed arrangement. Here is this prince of yours, starting the journey of his life absolutely directionless and purposeless, not concerned about his life or his family's honour," his father said.

His mother pleaded, "Stop blaming him now. We will discuss it later once he is out of his current state of shock."

*

Next morning Daman headed straight for his school and to his favourite spot, his ears reverberating with his parents' heated debate of the previous night and his mother's pleas.

There were very few people in the school, now closed after the end of the academic year.

The palash tree looked drier with a few birds hopping among its branches and feasting on the remaining blooms. The dance of the dry leaves no longer soothed his mind. Their falling seemed to be like a death in disgrace.

Daman sat there looking at the dry leaves and drew on the ground a group of stars with a dry stick.

"Drawing stars on the ground won't change your fortune, friend. These stars aren't for poor people like you or me. They shine only for the select few." Daman, startled by this interruption, looked up to find Sanga standing near him. Daman looked at him in surprise and quickly wiped out the stars he had drawn.

Sanga kneeled down beside him, staring at his drawings. "Don't get surprised, I was talking to my friends nearby when I saw you walk in. Let's go for a walk along the river," he said, putting his arms around Daman's shoulder.

"You'll feel better."

This exhibition of sympathy brought tears to Daman's eyes and he followed Sanga, mesmerised by his presence and extended hand of friendship.

Sanga said, "I'd also dreamed of pursuing a respectable career, but in this country people like you and me have no right to dream. So I didn't bother to sit for these exams. Why sit in these false exams and wait for this government-orchestrated result to inform me of failure? I chose the path of revolution and sacrifice, so that one day somebody like you or me could get his rights."

Sanga looked into Daman's big eyes as he spoke and finding no trace of disbelief, he continued, "I vowed to reform this system and many friends have joined me since in this quest for truth. We seek to expose the corrupt reality of our existing system and find means to create a new system which delivers justice for people like you, so that we can also dream." He talked on and on.

Daman started to internalise this philosophy, perceiving it as a small light at the end of the very dark tunnel of his gloomy thoughts.

Both of them were by now deep into the wilderness spreading around the river. They had followed a jeep track made along the Barkha river, mainly used by the farmworkers for local agricultural activities. The prevailing dry season and siphoning of water through multiple small drains for the nearby farms had subdued the river's flow.

"Would you like to meet a few of my friends?" Sanga shot this question unexpectedly. Daman looked at Sanga without any expression of acceptance or rejection. The solemn silence that followed was broken by the rough pumping sounds of a motorcycle, which had stopped on the other side of the track towards the river. Two young men on it, wearing helmets, gestured frantically to Sanga, who rushed towards them.

Daman stayed on the other edge of the track, which sloped down twenty feet to the boundary of a big sugarcane field. The three of them continued an agitated discussion and the two riders repeatedly turned their heads backwards as if expecting somebody.

Suddenly, a volley of gunshots shattered the silence of the wilderness. The pillion rider collapsed, falling backwards. Sanga ran and quickly dived into the river. Further shots rang out and the sounds of a huge commotion came from behind the trees, a hundred metres away. The second person, pinned down by the fallen motorcycle, cursed loudly before closing his eyes.

Sanga swam away from the scene along the flow of the river, while Daman slid down the slope to the thick sugarcane field. The commotion, swearing and sounds of running in heavy police boots quickly grew closer. They converged around the fallen men and some pointed towards the direction Sanga had escaped down the river.

Daman walked away unnoticed through tall sugarcanes till he reached his school boundary. He walked past his dream landmarks again, the school bench and the palatial house, but failed to notice them. His mind was lost in the cobweb of recent events, which he failed to comprehend. He reached home and felt relieved to find his father was not back yet.

He quietly went inside his room and slipped into his bed. He lay there petrified, trying to understand the reality of what had happened.

"When did you come in, Daman?" his mother enquired.

His pallid looks alarmed her and she rushed to his side. "What's wrong, Daman?" she asked. She put her hand on his forehead. "Oh, God! You have a fever. Please tell me what's going on, Daman," she pleaded, constantly massaging his head.

"I'm fine, Ma, don't worry," he said, attempting in vain to reassure and comfort her.

"You are not going to move out of bed. I will bring you a glass of milk."

Daman looked at his mother, and wished he could hide in her maternal lap, forgetting his sorrows forever.

At that moment, his father returned from the office. Finding his wife sitting next to Daman, he enquired of her, "What is wrong?"

"His forehead is burning, he's not well," she wailed.

"For God's sake, don't spoil him further, we have already paid a big price for that. How can he feel better after destroying my lifelong dream? Just leave him alone and he will be fine. He has to learn now to live a life of misery, which is his fate and ours as well." He stamped out of the room, while Daman's frightened eyes followed his exit.

Sleep came again to Daman's rescue but brought with it oppressive dreams. He dreamed that he was walking in a sun-scorched desert with his father, and his foot became ensnared in a clawed trap. He cried for help, but his father was unable to hear his wailing and continued to pull him along.

*

The next day, he was woken up by his father's loud voice, commenting on an item in the morning newspaper. "Oh, God! What is happening to the youth of Barkhapur? Rather than working hard to improve their future, they are becoming terrorists and confronting the police. It is unbelievable that these young boys attacked a police jeep.

As a result, two are dead and one is missing, with police hotly pursuing him. I am sure this fellow is from Daman's school."

It was not difficult for Daman to guess what his father was ranting about. He grabbed the newspaper the moment his father left for his office. This was a local newspaper, which had carried the news of the riverside shootout in headlines and was full of accolades for the local police action, and their bravery in killing two dangerous terrorists.

There was also a photograph of Sanga under the caption, *"SOUGHT BY POLICE, THIS TERRORIST RAN AWAY AFTER A GUNFIGHT WITH THE POLICE"*. It gave the name of Inspector Krura as the contact for anyone providing any information.

Panic gripped Daman, with a sudden surge of intense fear of prosecution. The common sounds of people passing by or even the rustling of guava tree leaves in the backyard made him shiver, fearing the arrival of police. His paranoia slowly pushed him into a dark corner, making him a frightened prisoner. At times, a meek voice from within urged him to break the shackles of fear and approach the police with honest details.

However, he failed to gather enough courage to do so. Once or twice, he did manage to go to the gate of the police station but left after the sentry questioned him about his purpose for coming there.

The shooting incident was followed by wild rumours about Sanga, including the news of him having killed some people in the neighbouring town. Daman was slowly developing a sense of guilt, believing he had not done his duty towards society by coming clean to the police about the information he had.

His sense of duty one day finally brought him to the police station where he addressed the sentry and demanded to see Inspector Krura.

The sentry took him to Head Constable Dhan instead. "Sir, this boy came to the police station before but would not say what he wanted. Today he is demanding to see Krura Sahib.' He spoke reluctantly, fearing a rebuke from Dhan for wasting his time.

"I want to talk to the Inspector Sahib only," said Daman, trying to gather enough courage to look directly at Dhan, who was surprised to see an innocent-looking boy with his eyes full of fear.

"You can talk to me; I am a Senior Constable here, and our Sahib is busy," said Dhan with a mischievous gleam in his eye, showing betel-nut -stained teeth as he smiled at Daman.

Daman, though not satisfied, reluctantly dragged a chair in front of Dhan's table to get seated. Dhan, a dark and stocky man, had been standing behind his desk when Daman entered. He also sat down, his thick-armed wooden chair making a loud creaking sound as his big frame settled in.

The sentry was asked to bring two cups of tea and he offered one to Daman, who reluctantly accepted it. His hand shook vigorously as he carried the cup to his lips.

Dhan stole a glance at his shaking hand as he poured his own cup's contents into the saucer, cooling it. The lukewarm tea would not hurt his teeth, decayed from constant betel-nut chewing.

He gave Daman a questioning look, as if demanding a quick start to his statement. Daman initially fumbled with his words but soon narrated the whole story without hiding any facts.

The Constable rose from his seat and patted Daman's back, his trademark mischievous smile playing on his face. He told Daman to stay seated while he informed Inspector Krura about him. He was back soon and told Daman in a very reassuring way to go home and not worry about a thing. This gave Daman the much sought-after relief he had hoped for from his visit to the police station.

But before he could walk out of that room, Krura walked in. He was a tall man with a stern look and a big moustache. He casually looked at Daman and asked Dhan to get his signed statement, home address and other details.

Daman walked home after giving these details wondering why the Inspector should seek this information after Dhan had reassured him about his position.

*

The terrorism news stayed in the top columns of most newspapers for the next few days as there had been attempts by the terrorist group to attack local police stations. This caused an intense political debate about the whole episode and created great pressure to catch the culprits. There was also pressure on the State Minister to resign due to the worsening law-and-order situation as more and more sabotage activities were reported.

The local police were also coming under intense pressure to produce results and catch the offenders. Their jobs were on the line if no breakthrough came. Sanga had become a household name by now and posters declaring a reward for his capture were displayed everywhere.

Daman had by now drifted into a stage of complete detachment, spending more and more of his time sleeping. He had lost weight and sank into a vegetative form of existence, devoid of all pleasurable activities. Perhaps this state of abandonment was his submission to the inevitable, or a mere adoption of a frame of mind which ignores all signals that would otherwise cause tremendous stress.

*

One morning, after his father had gone to work, Dhan came calling and asked Daman to accompany him to the police station for an urgent matter.

Inspector Krura greeted Daman with an affectionate smile and took him inside his room. Dhan stood at the door while the Inspector addressed Daman. "I called you here because there is bad news for you. We have information that terrorists have come to know about your visit to the police station and they are planning to take revenge. We have a responsibility to protect you."

Daman was unmoved; his state of mind helped him to not react to this threat.

Sensing how little impact Krura's word had on him, Dhan interjected, attempting to reinforce the message. "Boy, do you understand the gravity of the situation or not? These are dangerous people."

"Shut up Dhan, don't try to scare this simple boy. It is our duty to protect him even if it means losing our lives."

"What should I do, Sir?" Daman had by now started to develop faith in Krura's words.

"Come with us," said Krura, and he ordered Dhan to take out his jeep; the Constable made a quick exit to comply.

Soon, the three of them were on the road leading to a thick jungle spread along the small hills surrounding Barkhapur. After about an hour's drive, they reached a deserted tube-well room, which had been used years ago to irrigate nearby – now deserted – vegetable farms. There were no signs of human habitation in the vicinity, just wilderness.

"Daman, you will have to live here for the next two to three days. During this time, we will be able to liquidate Sanga and his gang to ensure your safe return home. Dhan will inform your family about your wellbeing and you do not have to worry about that," said Inspector Krura, with his arms around Daman's shoulders. "Supplies for your daily needs have been carefully stocked here, including a small kerosene stove. One of us will visit you daily to ensure your wellbeing."

"But why do I have to stay in this wilderness, why not in my house under police protection?" This was the first time Daman had picked up enough courage to reason with them.

"You should not be asking silly questions like that. Let us do our duty. Don't you have faith in our commitment towards your security?" Inspector Krura said in a stern voice, staring at him.

"Sir, what about a weapon for his protection?" said Dhan to Krura as they walked away.

"Oh yes! Get that revolver from the jeep and also some ammunition for Daman's use," said the Inspector.

"Have you ever used a gun?" enquired Dhan, with his ugly, mischievous smile, as he handed over a rusty country-made revolver to Daman.

Daman was once again deep into his state of detachment and had no idea what was going on. He robotically accepted the gun and mumbled, "Sir, I have no idea how to use this. Why should I need this anyway?"

"Do not argue, son; just do what you're told. We are doing our best for your wellbeing, that's all. I will teach you how to use it, which is very simple," said Krura, holding Daman's right hand with the revolver and forcing his index finger towards the trigger.

He suddenly jerked Daman's right arm up and squeezed his finger.

A shot was fired, shaking Daman's small frame. Krura repeated this manoeuvre. Another shot broke the silence of the wilderness, resulting in the sounds of squealing and fluttering of wings from many birds taking flight from their resting positions in the surrounding trees.

"Don't you ever say you can't shoot," said Krura, as he grinned at Daman admiringly.

"We will leave you now, and please close the door of this room when you go in."

*

Once the sound of the police jeep had died down Daman went inside the room and inspected the contents. He was surprised to see it reasonably well-stocked with food. There were loaves of bread, eggs and even milk in a container. There was also a small cot with reasonable bedding and a blanket. The room seemed to have been used, at least sparingly, in the past few weeks.

He came out and looked around. There were bushes growing around the room and thick forest surrounding it on all sides. The soft wind flowing through the jungle rustled the leaves, sounding like water flowing in a wild stream. Daman found a patch of smooth grass to lie on under the clear view of the blue sky. He looked at the sky and caught sight of a group of eagles flying at a great height. They flew in a circle following each other. Daman admired and envied their freedom. He did, however, find much-needed peace in this solitude.

He had now learned to flow with the stream of life and to abandon his struggle of swimming against its current. Surprisingly he was not afraid anymore and felt proud about it.

His dreams had started to return and he once again thought about Rima. He wondered whether there was still an opportunity for him to be with her. He also thought about his mother and how she would cope with his absence.

The next three days passed and he had one police visitor every day to give him assurance and supplies.

Daman was by now becoming homesick.

On the fourth day, just after sunset, a police jeep came, carrying two armed policemen along with Krura and Dhan. They stopped about two hundred metres away from the tube-well room. The sun had just gone below the horizon and the shadows of the tall surrounding trees had started to grow long.

Krura came up to Daman and asked, "Daman, get your revolver and show me whether you can still shoot or not. Walk away from me towards your room door and shoot in the air. If you are able to do so we will be assured of your skills to protect yourself in your own house." Krura continued to walk back while giving these instructions.

Daman was surprised by this awkward request but the prospect of going back home blinded him. He did exactly what Krura had told him.

Once he had fired three shots in the air, Krura took out his gun and pumped two bullets into his back. Daman collapsed, falling forward on his face, just inside the door of that room. A flash of a light and the eagles flying in a burning sky were his last visions.

*

The next day, newspapers in Barkhapur carried headlines about a shootout in the forest between terrorists and the police. One accomplice of the terrorists was reported killed while another, possibly Sanga, got away. Police had success in discovering and destroying a terrorist hideout near an abandoned tube-well.

There was a photograph of Daman's dead body on display in the local police station with a police contingent standing behind it. A revolver and five empty bullet cartridges were displayed next to the body.

Krura stood proudly in the front with the pride of a job well done written all over his face. Dhan, standing in the back row, was photographed attempting to squeeze his burly frame in front of his fellow policemen, doing his best to not miss an opportunity of getting his share of the limelight. His face carried his trademark mischievous smile.

* * *

The Last Salute

They had gathered early in the morning in front of Colonel Tanvir Saxi's home, standing huddled together on the side of a dusty road, anxiously waiting for him to come out. "Come! Join the early morning show!" They greeted every newcomer, in loud, animated voices.

The word had spread through the local children about a Colonel who had recently moved here, and the item of interest was his peculiar moustache.

The prying game they had stumbled upon provided their innocent minds, made idle by the long days of their summer holidays, with a novel excitement, and no one wanted to be left out.

The sun rose in the sky like a golden fireball tossed up from the horizon and started to pour its lava on the city with increasing ferocity. However, it failed to dissuade the young adventurers.

The rusty clatter of a bicycle bell momentarily distracted them and their eyes followed a newspaper boy who appeared in a flash from one end and dextrously threw a rolled newspaper into the front lawn of the Colonel's house, before disappearing in haste. The loud thud brought an order in that assembly, galvanised by the prospect of the imminent arousal of the Colonel by that stimulus.

True to their expectations, Colonel Saxi soon came out to pick up the newspaper. In silence they squirmed together, trying to reduce their collective mass to stay out of sight of the Colonel's sleepy eyes.

"Oh! It's really big!' exclaimed one child in a hushed voice. "It almost touches his ears on both sides," he continued, his mouth partly open in awe and amazement.

"Shh-shh! Shut up! Don't make loud sounds. He will notice us," worried another.

Unaware of his young admirers, the Colonel stepped down from his verandah onto the dry lawn. Standing close to where the newspaper lay, he stretched his tall frame and slowly lifted his sleep-weary eyes, adjusting them to the bright daylight. His eyes roved around, as they would have done when inspecting his battalion. He inspected the flowerbeds skirting the lawn, neatly punctuated by saplings, which had mostly wilted in the prevailing heat. He felt let down by those plants, who he believed had failed in their duty, like uninspired soldiers, to blossom quickly and provide a decorative look to the garden.

Two crows sat on the front wall, keeping a close watch on the Colonel's eye and body movements. As he descended into his garden, he met their gaze, and this made the crows take off with loud and enraged cawing, incensed by the threat to their liberty to search for food. Unconcerned by the protesting crows, the Colonel's gaze now travelled beyond the wall to his old Fiat parked on the street, then on to the group of children, standing close together in a row at the other end.

Excited by this visual connection, one of the children, standing in front, imitated a military salute. Another, standing behind him, mischievously slapped the back of his head and pushed him away from the group. The Colonel smiled back and the children, excited by their mission accomplished, ran away, happily chanting:

"Army General gets a salute,
Poor sepoy gets the boot!"

The commotion frightened the indignant crows from their safe refuge in a tree, directly above the children. They emerged to shoot into the bright summer air, protesting loudly and angrily, flapping their wings wildly.

The Colonel picked up the newspaper and went inside, pleased with the vibrant life around him and the impact he felt he directly made on its existence.

*

A long career as a commanding officer in the army had changed him, making him develop an exacting personality. However, this was punctuated by occasional fits of impetuosity. His demanding attitude and domineering moustachioed looks did limit his social circle, but he continued to maintain his friendship with a small group of elite army officers.

The Colonel was very fond of certain items he had collected in his lifetime, which included awards from his polo games and a medal awarded for his supreme bravery shown during a battle. He valued these more than his other possessions, and always enthusiastically showed them off to his visitors.

Preet, his wife, was a very different person. She had a sweet nature, with a temperament that persevered in the face of any adversity. She would on many occasions act as her husband's modest adviser, especially during times of any misdemeanours on his part, while trying her best to be not too censorious and hurt the enormous ego of a successful army officer. This usually helped to moderate the course of events whenever a vehement act of her husband took a nasty turn, thereby avoiding a possible catastrophe.

With their children successfully settled in their professions, as a decent elderly couple after a life of service and sacrifice, they had just begun living their dream of retirement in this new three-bedroom house in a quiet suburb of Delhi. They had already made the advance payment for their house, while the rest was due within one month. The Colonel expected his gratuity, saved over years of his army service, to cover the final payment.

"Preet, I look forward to the final settlement and the day we'll get the papers for the ownership of our house," he said.

He had said this almost every day to his wife, eager to finish the deal. It worried him that a stumbling block might fall in the way of their dream's realisation.

*

Another matter that intrigued them, since their arrival in this house, was the behaviour of the local children. They were unable to guess the reason behind the children's attention and thought this to be either simple curiosity about them as new arrivals, or a naive effort on their part to introduce themselves.

The Colonel personally believed – mistakenly – that their curiosity related to the fame he had gained by winning the bravery award. The real reason for children's interest, in fact, was the well-groomed moustache on the Colonel's florid face. The moustache was indeed a special one, not only in size, extending as it did from his lips to his sideburns, but also having sentimental significance.

Three years ago, he had changed it from a thin pencil moustache to its present size just before receiving his bravery award on Republic Day for his role on the Western Front during the war. Whenever he looked at his majestic moustache, it brought to his mind that special day, filling him instantly with pride. That day marked an important milestone in his life.

*

The heat of the day continued to grow with the rising sun, forcing the birds to seek refuge back in the thick shade of the tree.

The Colonel came out again after few hours. This time he was dressed elegantly in his army uniform, defying the midday heat, all his war medals adorning his proud chest. He had dressed to look impressive while presenting himself and dealing with the relevant officer in the accounts office. He was going there to be paid his gratuity.

He was surprised to see that group of local children again, braving the heat. They stood in a row with their arms wrapped around each other's shoulders on the other side of the street. Once they realised that the Colonel was looking at them, they mischievously turned their faces away with a chuckle, pretending they had never looked at him. One of them, perhaps more faint-hearted than his fellows, awed by Colonel's military finery, made a sudden dash away, while the others chased him, screaming, laughing and singing in unison,

"Coward! Coward! Gives a rant,

Sees a General, pisses in his pants…"

The Colonel smiled faintly, more confident now than ever that it was his striking appearance that attracted them to him, or perhaps created fear in their hearts.

He opened his car's front door and sat inside in the driver's seat. As his car rolled forward with a hoarse growl the kids returned to chase the car, singing and screaming in joy. They competed with each other to touch the moving body of the car, not concerned by the bellowing smoke of the old engine or the ochre dust rising from the road.

*

The office he was going to was in a shopping area and located on the first floor, with a row of expensive showrooms underneath. The stairs leading to the office area were dark and dusty, starting from a broad cemented verandah in front of the showrooms. This covered verandah housed many stall-owners, selling everything from tea and snacks to fruits like guavas and bananas. They sat on their haunches in the shade, smoking and gossiping and intently observing the passers-by.

The appearance of the sumptuously dressed Colonel Saxi attracted their immediate attention. The banana seller and a tea-stall owner stood up, awed by his looks, greeting him ceremoniously with folded hands. The Colonel, true to his attitude, gave them a faint, dignified smile and a small nod. He then strode up the stairs, ignoring their rapt attention.

At the end of these stairs, just inside the entrance door, sat a peon in a dirty khaki uniform, with an identity badge on his chest that displayed his name, "Guman". He sat on a four-legged wooden stool, humming a song from a popular Bollywood movie and crushing tobacco in his palm to make a roll.

Guman looked up at Colonel without showing any awe at the sight of a formally dressed army officer. He shot a question, "Whom do you want to see?

The Colonel was amazed by his attitude, and attributed his behaviour to his being a mere simpleton, unable to comprehend the significance of his rank or army decorations.

"Where's the office of Mr Besur, who's in charge of high-ranking army officers' post-retirement entitlements? I've an appointment to see him," he said, stressing "high-ranking army officer" to send a strong message to the dimwit.

To his astonishment, Guman was still unimpressed and continued his pill-rolling movement. Without bothering to look at the Colonel, he said, "Take that seat. Mr Besur is out for his morning tea and should be back soon."

The Colonel looked at the seat he was offered and was shocked to find a stool similar to the one Guman was sitting on, which would not have withstood the weight of his heavy frame.

His wandering eyes soon located a door bearing the name of Mr Besur.

"I'll wait for Mr Besur in his office," he announced, walking into the office without waiting for Guman's response.

He waited almost an hour, sitting impatiently in a chair in front of a big wooden table littered with dirty looking files, idly twitching his fingers. Then he heard a sudden commotion and the sound of quick steps coming upstairs, followed by the sound of Guman's wooden stool scraping the floor, as he stood up to show his respect for his approaching boss.

A short and stocky person soon entered the cabin where the Colonel sat, trying to cool his agitated nerves.

The man ignored the Colonel. He called out to Guman, while frantically looking for a file in the big heap on the table. "Guman, what the hell are you doing outside! Find that bloody file of General Sahib."

"Coming, Sahib," came an abrupt reply, and Guman was there in no time. He shuffled through the files, ignoring the Colonel, who was sitting there in a state of amazement, not knowing what to do.

Soon Guman fished out the desired file, handed it over to Mr Besur and informed him of the presence of the Colonel in his room.

Besur stole a look at Colonel but did not acknowledge him or show any respect. The Colonel lost his patience. He stood up, a tall and imposing figure in front of a short and stubby Besur, and puffed his chest as if to attract his attention to his army decorations.

He spoke in a stern voice, "Mr Besur, you had fixed a time to meet me, which was an hour ago. And here you are not even bothering to acknowledge my presence."

He tried his best not to let his voice shake with disgust, though by the end of his sentence he had started to quiver with rage and was on the verge of an explosion.

During this outburst he had a good look at Besur's face, and his expression changed from angry to surprise.

Besur had a strange, chubby baby-like face with deep sadness set in his eyes, but a happy smile hovering on his lips. This odd combination of expressions surprised the Colonel. He felt guilty for being rude to such a person, though he was not sure whether Besur deserved these sentiments.

While the Colonel stood, perplexed, Besur interjected, "What can I do for you, Sir?" He did not apologise nor show any bewilderment as he spoke.

"I'm Colonel Saxi and I called you a few days ago to arrange for my gratuity payment."

"Sir, I had ordered your file to be transferred from the Army Head Office long ago but unfortunately it has not arrived as yet." Besur continued to be very calm, adding to the Colonel's astonishment.

The Colonel wondered how a man with such childish features and sad eyes could retain such calm and not worry when dealing with a decorated officer such as himself. He failed to retain his own calm, and spoke in a tone heavy with suppressed rage, "When do you want me to come again? Will you make sure that my next visit is not wasted?"

Besur looked up again at him, shot a sad smile and said in a reassuring tone, as if consoling a child, "Please come back after two weeks; your work will be done."

The Colonel was taken aback by the unhelpful response. In a continued display of resentment, he said, "You don't understand, Mr Besur. I'll be thrown out of my house if I don't pay my dues in the next four weeks."

"Sir, I've given you my word, please come back after two weeks," Besur said, still maintaining his cool.

On his return home, the Colonel, contrary to his usual habit of loudly declaring his presence to Preet, quietly sneaked into his room. Preet knew all was not well and decided not to prod him. She also decided not to inform him about the receipt of another reminder about the impending payment.

At dinner, Preet finally asked him, "Tanvir, how was your first experience with a civil administration office?" She had tried to approach the topic laterally rather than questioning the success of his visit.

"It was all right. I've to go back after two weeks to finish the job," the Colonel said, not looking at her as he spoke.

Preet did not probe the topic further, and said, "I invited the young children inside – you know the ones who always hang around our house. I gave them some sweets, while they quietly sat under our verandah and introduced themselves."

The Colonel by now had been able to put aside the memory of his encounter with the clerk, and looked admiringly at her, showing special interest in the information about the children.

"Do you know, they're as young as eight to ten years old? I must admit they are all polite, and also natural inquisitors." Preet was happy she had brought about a change in the Colonel's mood.

*

The Colonel's next visit to the office was no different, though Besur gave him a welcoming smile, which surprised him. Besur took out an old dusty file, which obviously had been received from the head office by now. On the front page were the Colonel's identification details with a six-year-old photograph, without his trademark moustache.

Besur turned the file to face him and, looking into his eyes, spoke in a grim voice, "We've a problem, sir! I am sure even you will not vouch that you look like the person shown in this photograph."

The Colonel was dumbstruck. A shiver ran down his spine. He could see that the photograph was an outdated one, especially because of the dramatic change brought about by his new look; he became convinced that this was being used to victimise him or to extract a bribe.

"What do you expect me to do, Mr Besur? We all change looks with time, that does not mean we lose our identity. My signatures are the same and I can bring witnesses to prove my identity." The Colonel had an initial surge of anger and this was evident in the first sentence he spoke. But he soon realised the futility of this emotion and subdued his voice, changing his tone to one of meek submission in the end.

"That is exactly what you need to do, sir, prove your identity, not to me, but on an affidavit in a magistrate's court." Besur was cool and unmoved. "Bring back that affidavit and your cheque will be handed over."

Besur put on an appeasing smile, before the Colonel's departure, and pointing to his photograph shot a question, "Sir! Can you dare say the person in this photograph is you? How can I hand over a cheque worth such a huge amount without proper verification?"

The Colonel clearly understood by now that any further argument with him was futile, and abruptly left his cabin.

His sullen exit through the stall-owners clearly revealed his state of mind to them. He could see that most of them had by now overcome the initial respect they held for him. The tea-stall owner had gathered enough courage to make a cheeky comment, "Sahib, you need a strong cup of tea from me to get through your dealings with this office." Obviously, they were familiar with the situation faced by most customers coming to this office.

*

The Colonel took Preet with him to the courts the next day, but a surprise awaited them. The courts were closed for the next four weeks, for the summer break.

He went back to Besur in an attempt to persuade him to release his payment, but he refused to relent.

"Sir! You should understand. All you need to do is grease Mr Besur's palm and your work will be done immediately," whispered Guman with a small smile on his lips as the Colonel passed him. But the self-respecting Colonel disregarded his proposal as despicable.

*

As the days went by, the Colonel's mind slowly sank into a state of turmoil; the respect he had seen during his army days was nowhere to be seen in his civil dealings. He felt more and more obliged to use Preet as a mediator between him and the civil system.

For the Colonel, with his combative spirit, this passive wait was like prolonged misery.

Preet tried her best to resurrect his old confidence and vigour, when he could take such uncertainties in his stride. But the baby-faced clerk haunted the Colonel. He could not believe that such an innocent-looking man could create such anxiety within him.

Preet's constant efforts to comfort him only partially succeeded and he blamed the civil system and its prevailing corruption as the reason for his present woes.

While the Colonel itched for a quick retaliatory action against the clerk, Preet dissuaded him, urging restraint. She was aware of her husband's possibly impulsive and overreaching response to the present situation, which at the worst could result in a temporary eviction for them.

"There is no battlefield here, Tanvir," she told him, "and you have no visible offending enemy either. What you face here is a group of social and economical losers. Remember you cannot win from a loser."

At times, the Colonel felt he could neither face nor talk to Preet about this issue, afraid he might lose his temper or worse, break down, especially if she said a word of sympathy or looked at him tenderly. He was possessed by moods of melancholy, with dark feelings of self-distrust, expressed through his agitated manner. He no longer felt proud of himself in front of the mirror, and his moustache reminded him of his baby-faced nemesis.

One evening, in a desire to do something, he shaved off his moustache and presented himself to Preet, quivering in indignation.

Her initial response was a sudden, stony silence, but this she abruptly overcame in an effort to provide much-needed comfort to her love. "You look much younger and this reminds me of our past days of fun!" she said, a faint smile on her face. "And who would refuse your payment now?"

The next day, when the Colonel went out once more to see Mr Besur, in a civil dress and without his moustache, his usual attendant band of children were dismayed and silent. Then came the low-pitched giggles, and a new chorus, slowly mounting to a crescendo.

"Uncle Saxi had a mouchhe,
Robbers came, stole the bush..."
They then disappeared into narrow byways.

*

The Colonel's appearance as he approached the office shocked the vendors, who sat as if frozen, taking time out of their routine activities to measure the gravity and impact of this unexpected sight.

Guman showed no reaction again, failing to notice this singular change and managed only a sheepish smile, perhaps from the guilt and fear of his previous comments.

Mr Besur's response was more dramatic than expected. His happy facial lines vanished instantly, leaving him with an expression of total sadness. He felt defeated, and without a word prepared an authority for the Colonel's withdrawal of gratuity funds from the bank. He quietly handed that over to an expressionless Colonel.

When the Colonel returned home, Preet's questioning eyes greeted him. Without saying a word, he took out the letter of authority and placed it on a nearby table.

He then went and slouched in a nearby lounge chair, his hands covering his face. It was as if he did not want Preet to look at that piece of paper and his changed appearance at the same time.

Preet looked at the paper and then at the concealed face of her husband. She tried to hold back her tears, but could not. She did not know what the tears were for: the joy of an accomplished job or grief over her husband's emotional trauma. Nevertheless, they flowed down her cheeks, purifying her mind and washing out the memories of the previous days of anguish.

The Colonel looked up, as if instinctively knowing that she was crying. He spoke in a mellowed voice, "Preet, your tears will wash away your sorrows and agony. How will the hurt in the heart of a decorated soldier go? A bravery award winner is not supposed to cry!"

"Tears are not a sign of weakness, Tanvir, and also not an escape from an agony. They are to bring an adjustment in your life by either celebrating a new achievement or coming to terms with your loss. Don't we cry both in happiness and sorrow?" Preet spoke even as the tears continued to flow down her cheeks.

She came up to him and grabbed his hand, dragging him out of *their* house to restart their routine of evening walks in the quiet lanes of their suburb.

* * *

Forgotten Sunrise

As soon as the mist cloaking the eastern hills cleared and the sun began to pour gold over our leafy suburb, a swarm of early morning ramblers appeared. Most of them came from the western end of my street, heading east to a natural reserve. Young, old, single or in pairs, dressed in multicoloured track pants and tops of various styles, they strode brightly into the glowing sunlight. Some ran and jogged, appearing to be in a hurry. Others walked leisurely, taking in the sights and sounds.

I owned a coveted position to observe all this – a house with a balcony, right on that street, surrounded by wilderness. I would stand there daily after grabbing a mug of steaming coffee.

This street, winding like a serpent through our neighbourhood, dipped steeply about two hundred metres from where I stood. This created a well-illuminated stage-like look on my western side, decorated on both sides by lush vegetation. A Christmas bush or rather a small tree, with its perennial coat of green leaves, proudly dominated that landscape. The early morning frost would deposit hundreds of tiny dewdrops on its leaves: precariously balanced, with the sunrays trapped inside, they glittered like pearls. True to its name, this gave the bush the appearance of a decorated Christmas tree. Alas, the rising warmth and light would soon melt the exhibition away.

Meanwhile the performance being played on that stage would continue to unfold. In our small leafy suburb, all characters in that drama had their signature personalities and backgrounds, which I learned more and more through our neighbourhood gossip.

I was perpetually fascinated by this show, and by all the participating characters. I could never figure out why it fascinated me so much to watch these people from my balcony. It could be that as an old man in his seventies living a retired single life, I drew delight in visions of vibrant life around me. A strange relationship had developed between us over time, though not easy to define. I never knew them personally, but they slowly became a family for me.

I particularly became very fond of Ron and his small dog, a white poodle called Ruff. They both lived down the sleepy street, not far from my house. Ron, also a seventy-plus retiree, always walked with slow, distinctively majestic steps, patient enough to stop as and when Ruff wanted his sniffing breaks. His age had apparently failed to wear him down, allowing him to live proudly through his sunset days. As they say, as you grow old your confidence grows, fed by the conviction that you are now more skilled to live than before.

Ron's appearance showed that conviction. His well-groomed hair, streaked with elegant grey, enhanced his grace. The lines on his weathered face, visible marks of his life's experiences, made him look tough and mature. What I liked most about him was the subtle, constant smile that played on his face, like a perpetual greeting for all. With his restive dog, held securely on a long leash, they seemed to be very happy partners, content within their own world.

As they walked on the roadside, Ruff's curious nostrils sniffed furiously at everything, as if to prevent an alien intrusion into their private world. He was particularly suspicious of the Christmas tree's dense growth: its low-growing branches, almost touching the ground, created a mysterious dead space underneath. Ruff seemed convinced it housed a stowaway animal, possibly a possum. These were notoriously rampant in our suburb.

His furious but fruitless search, accompanied by growling and scratching, lasted fifteen to twenty minutes each day. Ron, amused by this, patiently looked on, feebly trying to control his agitated mate and the slipping leash. Once done with his snooping, still full of energy, Ruff pulled Ron forward, challenging his old teak-hard frame. Maintaining his balance by arching his body backwards, Ron would trundle along.

They both enjoyed this as much as I did; their daily walk was never a mundane exercise. At times Ron would stop in front of my house, exchange pleasantries with me. I viewed this as an attempt to bond with another single person living alone. He also seemed to like my passive participation in the sunrise moments but never invited me to join him. Perhaps he didn't want to share this precious time with a third person.

As the sun rose higher, diminishing the roadside shadows, they would meander along, undiminished in their enthusiasm and then disappear, only to be seen again the next morning.

I would often think about them and wonder how my day would be without this show. That unfortunate day came soon enough.

*

One day, soon after the sun had brightened the road corner, I started looking for my ramblers as usual. One after another, all the characters appeared, young and old, all with their signature style, but not Ron and Ruff. My eyes waited for them, but in vain. The sun continued its slow journey to the west, making me more and more anxious. Nothing changed.

I faced similar disappointments for the next few days.

I made enquiries and soon found out that Ron's wife, totally unknown in our neighbourhood, had left him. To make it worse, she apparently took Ruff with her! I was surprised to know that Ron and Ruff shared their small world with another person. Not knowing the nature of the relationship Ron had with his wife, my immediate concern was Ron's welfare without Ruff. This thought made me very restless over the next few days.

*

After nine long days of waiting, Ron reappeared. The timing was immaculate, the sunshine was spot on, but his beloved companion was gone. He looked miserable and lost. The lines of toughness on his face had faded. His eyes lacked the usual spark, as if the essence of his life had been scooped out of those sockets.

He walked with a shuffle, totally oblivious to his surroundings, holding the rolled-up dog leash like an old treasure. In the extremities of life we switch back to the basics and our memories become our most valuable possessions. This was what seemed to be happening to Ron.

He slowed down and stopped next to the Christmas bush. He stood there for a moment, staring at it and then slowly sank to his knees beside it. His eyes searched intently for something there, but he abandoned his search abruptly, with visible frustration. He threw his head back, rose and stood uncertainly for a while before reluctantly stepping back. Looking defeated, he turned and walked away in the direction from which he had come. That was totally different from his routine in the past.

As the days went by, I could see a dramatic change within him. He seemed to be ageing by the day. He never raised his gaze to look at me. That lovable sublime smile he wore in the past had vanished. Slowly, his morning appearances grew shorter and became limited to the bush. He spent more and more time beside the bush, as if he had lost his sense of time. It seemed to me that he hoped that one day Ruff would wriggle out from under there.

I was getting very worried about his state of mind. However, I couldn't gather enough courage to interact with him because his body language was clearly screaming "Leave me alone!"

One day, to my amazement, the old pair emerged from their corner again, welcomed, as always, by the morning light. I heaved a sigh of relief – my visual delights were back. They both looked equally aged and worn out, reduced to just a shadow of their old selves. They lacked the vibrant energy that had been so palpable in the past. Though I knew their reunion would begin to rejuvenate them soon, the change in their personas was obvious.

Ruff seemed to have forgotten his past rituals and adventures. He did not go sniffing for any intrusions, nor did he go close to the Christmas bush. He didn't pull Ron forward, but gently walked besides him. He constantly sniffed Ron's legs to make sure he was still there, something he must have been desperately searching for during their days of separation and loneliness.

I came to know later that Ruff, soon after his relocation, ran away from his new home. Searching for Ron, hungry and dehydrated, he had travelled more than a hundred miles and triumphantly found his soulmate. Their long separation had definitely taken its toll. Though they both looked physically and emotionally drained, I knew for sure that their healing process had now begun.

My smile was back. I turned away from my balcony, sipped my now cold coffee, and realised how important their companionship had been for me as well.

Their early morning appearances once again started to light my face with a smile, even more so now.

* * *

Vanishing Frontiers

Badly injured, I struggled to lean over him. His eyes were half closed with face bearing a pleading look. He seemed to be only dimly conscious of himself as his parched tongue sluggishly licked his dry lips.

I had just shot him in the stomach half an hour ago, when he leaned over me either to check whether I was alive, or to snatch my possessions. Shot, he had sunk just next to me in a heap. He must have been disappointed to find me alive after his vicious grenade attack on my jeep had catapulted me some distance away.

I noticed how his gaze was fixed on my water bottle. His eyes begged for a precious drop. The lucky bottle, securely fastened to my waist, had somehow survived the impact of the blast.

I tried to remove the bottle from my waist. It required some effort on my part. The fingers that came away holding the bottle were moist and sticky with blood.

I thrust the bottle towards him. *Was I rewriting the laws of war?*

I knew our destiny and the outcome no longer mattered as a win or a loss. The hatred he had surely nursed in his heart when he flung that grenade no longer showed in his eyes.

Gathering his remaining energy, he grabbed the bottle in a flash and quickly gulped the contents down, spilling half into the thirsty sand of the vast desert. He gave back a faint smile of thanks. I winked, acknowledging his gratitude, knowing well that I had just deprived myself of my only possible lifeline.

His eyes were slowly closing; I knew his time had come. I turned my face away.

The sand I lay on was fast losing heat with the setting sun. My body was getting colder. The metallic stench of our spilled blood mixed with the burning explosives around us covered me like a shroud.

Left alone after losing my last hostile companion, my thoughts were now aimless, as were my eyes as they searched the depths of that alien night sky. My eyes tried searching for my favourite stars – I had loved looking at them in my childhood. All in vain.

The silence around made me vulnerable. Nothing moved; the surrounding stillness was frightful. I hoped for some divine intervention to break this silence and bring back the signs of life. But even as my wide-open eyes continued their search, nothing changed. The only source of light, sound and warmth was my burning jeep, now engulfed in flames, extinguishing my last hopes.

My body writhed in pain, yearning for a caring embrace or even a simple, friendly touch. Time slowed down, as if to mercifully extend the prospect of a saviour's arrival – a futile desire that I knew would never materialise. My troubled thoughts and desires were being unceremoniously dumped into the depths of a fathomless black hole.

The strange stars in the dark sky stared back at me.

*

I held a fistful of sand, desperately seeking the familiar feel of the moist soil of the garden of my childhood home in Rupnagar. My small hands had loved squeezing the wet clay soil, feeling it escape from between my fingers. I did the same to that handful of sand, which slowly slipped out from between the gaps between my feeble fingers. A last-ditch effort to keep a grasp on my life was failing. Tired and weary, the flames from the burning jeep, as well as my desires, were slowly dying out. I was fast losing the last battle.

I felt a gentle shake on my shoulders. My wife was trying to wake me up without giving me a fright. I had no desire to wake up. I started to embrace the slumber that was taking my desires away, as a steady stream of tender feelings filled the void. I sensed blessings and fulfilment surge within my body. I was left with the smoothness of her gentle touch. I did not let it go. I treasured it.

The strangeness of my surroundings was gradually becoming meaningless as I felt myself being assimilated into that sand. Surprisingly, my pain and the unpleasantness of the hostile desert had also started to dissipate. The foreignness of the sky no longer threatened; the unfriendly stars now seemed to be forgiving and smiled back at me. I was becoming an integral part of this foreign land.

Magnanimous time stretched itself again, awarding me another precious moment to fly back to my childhood, and get my hands wet in my home soil again. I heard the sound of the roaring river that flowed near our house, felt a momentary moistening of my palms, and the rising mist enveloping my face. I heard distant voices, unrecognisable and directionless. Perhaps my old memories were calling me back.

As my slumber deepened, I no longer wished or waited for a caring touch or a saviour. Nothing carried meaning any more, neither my uniform nor the decorations that had proudly adorned my chest. The only path in front of my eyes seemed to be heading towards eternity, that boundless black space, for the final assimilation.

I knew there was no turning back now. Alone in this journey, I was no longer a soldier, nor was there any enemy. There was no war and no frontiers to conquer. I belonged everywhere and nothing belonged to me.

* * *

Death of a Tree God

The excitement was palpable. A small boy, clad in shorts, madly embraced a medium-sized sheesham tree as a thin dark man in a white dhoti struggled hard to rip his hands away. Standing not far from them was a short fat man in a shiny cream-coloured dhoti and kurta, urging the man to try harder. A curious group of local villagers surrounded them, with muted expressions.

Fat Lala's eyes spilled fire and his shaking body indicated he was raring to have a go himself. "Hira! You son of a bitch, haven't you eaten anything today? Why can't you tear his bloody hands apart?" he crowed.

Hira's hissing sounds became harsher, exhaling like blasts of sharp wind through his flared nostrils and clenched teeth. His thin facial muscles became tauter, as beads of sweat dripped down his face. His bony fingers writhed like agitated serpents, desperately attempting to reach between Babool's tiny hands and the rough tree bark. Their struggle shook the tree. With each shake, it shed its white-pink flowers onto the struggling bodies below, without discrimination. But neither Hira nor Lala were interested in the non-discriminatory gesture of the doomed tree.

Hira anchored his heels deeper into the ground to stabilise his tiring frame and reinforce his slippery grip. His body curved backwards, showing the neat rows of his ribs under his arched, heaving chest.

It was amazing how ten-year-old Babool managed to hold on to the tree with his undying resolve. He was on a mission to save the life of his friend, the tree, from the threat posed by Lala, a timber contractor. Soon the tiring gymnastics of Hira started to amuse the crowd of villagers watching. They giggled at the sight of his thin, lizard-like body writhing around Babool. They laughed at fat Lala's swaying dhoti and kurta as he jumped, every now and then, like a football referee, hands on his hips trying to secure his dhoti, his mouth wide open, revealing crooked teeth.

Lala's and Hira's tools, a rusted saw with wooden handles at both ends and a medium-sized axe, lay idle beside them. Both of them were getting more desperate by the minute. A pair of small hands was successfully defying their desperate attempts to get to their prey.

As the day wore on, the weary hands of Hira started to give up and Lala's hope began to fade. Sensing defeat, fat Lala looked at the amused crowd and agitatedly declared, "Don't worry! This is not the end. This tree is mine, and I'll take it soon!"

The crowd by now had started to laugh loudly.

"You will see! You will see!" he hissed under his breath, unable to gather enough courage to look at Babool, whose thin arms and small determined hands were the cause of his humiliating defeat.

Hira got the message and loosened his grip, his panting frame drenched in sweat, which he wiped with his loincloth and backed away from the tree and its saviour.

"Hooray!" a rousing ovation came from the crowd. Still Babool stood his ground, continuing to embrace the tree.

Slowly Lala, Hira and most of the crowd melted away, leaving only two boys, similar to Babool in age, staying back.

"He saved his friend," muttered one.

"It's strange that he is friends only with trees and plants. He never plays with us. Even my new toy cart hasn't interested him," lamented the other boy, raising his toy cart to demonstrate its bright colours, hoping it would catch Babool's eye.

Babool was not interested. He was deeply concerned about this particular tree. He knew Lala would be back within minutes of his departure, so he stood his ground, embracing his friend.

It was only when Mohan, his father, arrived, that he got separated from the tree. Mohan slapped Babool, forcefully ripped his hands away from the tree and dragged him towards their home. Fearful of Babool breaking free, Mohan made sure his grip around Babool's left arm stayed strong.

"You are not called Babool for nothing," lamented Mohan. "Your love for that wretched, thorny babool tree in our courtyard and your madness about all trees has only grown since the day you were born."

As the two of them headed towards their hut, he muttered, "I can't forget when you, as a two-year-old, hardly able to walk, would run crying like a wounded jackal whenever I tried to cut that evil babool tree. The tree that gave us nothing but a shower of sharp thorns and dried twigs in our small backyard."

Mohan continued to blabber as they walked, "I vividly remember the sounds of your ankle trinkets as you would run and your ear-piercing cries in response to my axe hitting that tree. I knew all those years ago that those were the signs of a coming storm."

"Your mother would follow, dropping whatever she held in her hands, worried you may hurt your feet on the scattered thorns. The result was that the damned tree survived and you got your name."

Mohan continued, knowing well that his words would have no effect on his son. "Oh God! Eight years on and yet the drama continues. We are going crazy. Nothing stands in your way whenever you get a whiff of a tree being cut."

They were now close to their one-room thatched house at the fringe of their small village of Amlala. The land that surrounded their house was mostly arid, albeit the sunset today had temporarily coated it with an illusionary ochre tinge.

For Mohan, ten-year-old Babool was their only wealth. Ironically his name came from the tree which stood in their courtyard, offering neither fruit nor shade, but periodically dropping thorny twigs on to the ground around it. This tree owed its life to Babool, its namesake.

*

Once home, Babool's mind continued to worry about his friend, the sheesham tree. He waited impatiently for his parents to go to sleep in order to sneak out of bed into the surrounding deep darkness.

It was a cold night made worse by a light drizzle. Undaunted, Babool rushed to his friend for he didn't want to be late. He knew Hira and Lala could be there any moment, taking advantage of the eerie night.

He immediately embraced the tree again and locked his fingers around it. His frail, barely covered body shivered violently. As expected, it wasn't long before Hira and Lala reappeared, draped in dark rubber raincoats this time.

"The little rascal is back again," ranted Lala.

"Let's see how long he holds on this time," screamed Hira.

"Don't waste time on him. Villagers may come back," snarled Lala.

He handed Hira the thick wooden stick he was holding. The message was clear. However, Babool made no noise, worried his father might come back.

Hira swung the stick and hit Babool's head hard. He slumped while his locked fingers kept their circle around the tree. Lala stared back at Hira, the message was clear again. Hira had another go. This blow was strong enough to make Babool unconscious; he fell backwards, releasing his beloved tree.

Lala gestured to Hira to pick up the boy's limp body and then they both disappeared in the nearby forest.

Lala told Hira, who was shaking with fright, "Don't worry, I have an idea."

*

When day broke, Mohan realised his son was missing. Frantically looking for him, he alarmed his wife, Radha. They ran around their house and paddock, then towards the village – but to no avail. Babool could not be found.

Mohan was the first to reach the spot where the sheesham tree once stood. It was gone, and the spot lay covered with its white-pink flowers.

He sank down in a heap, holding his head, as a shocked Radha joined him. Slowly, more and more villagers came and stood around.

A voice was heard, a hushed whisper, "The Tree God has disappeared!"

The crowd spoke in unison, "The Tree God has disappeared…"

The voice spoke again, stronger this time. "Yes, we didn't recognise that small soul was a Tree God. Alas, He left us along with His abode, the sheesham tree."

People turned to look at the person speaking. It was fat Lala, with a petrified Hira trying to hide behind his big frame.

Hira stepped out and fell on the ground. "The Tree God is dead," he whimpered.

Lala immediately intervened, "Perhaps we sinners didn't deserve to have a living God among us. And He left us," he spoke looking at the people standing around him.

"Let's now do our best to keep His memory alive. In order to bless this village and to worship Him, I hereby commit to construct here a small temple for our beloved Tree God."

Hira grovelled on the ground murmuring indistinctly "Do you think He will forgive me?"

Fat Lala ignored him and raised his fat arms to the skies. "That's God's command. A Tree God temple will be built here soon."

The villagers stood around mutely, hands folded, too overcome to move.

Mohan and Radha stayed on their knees, heads bowed, wordless; their dead eyes staring at the ground where the small feet of their Babool had once firmly stood.

* * *

My Home is in the Stars

(A night in a refugee camp, 1947)

The odd showers in late August had cleared the air of dust. This made visible a night sky littered with glittering stars. The moonless night and the enveloping darkness around this refugee camp in Punjab made the view extra luminous.

On the banks of the nearby River Sutlej, a hundred flickering fireflies floated and danced majestically in heavenly rhythm. Their celestial dance and its reflection in the river created a mirage effect every night, magically mirroring the image of the stars in the sky.

The monsoons had left a spread of mature vegetation around the camp, inviting the nocturnal activities of the local fauna. Seeking mates, they made calls of varying pitch throughout the night. The abundance of seasonal life also encouraged countless predators, including snakes. Feasting on each other, they killed not for hate but to faithfully participate in the task of maintaining the cycle of life and death as demanded by mother nature. A mild cool breeze and the aroma rising out of the warm soil as it cooled, could soothe even a troubled soul. Such a smell stays in one's memory forever.

The bounteous allure of nature, however, failed to elicit any interest from the inhabitants of this camp. Most newly arrived refugees chose to stay inside their poorly lit tents.

In a state of despair, they found some solace by huddling together with their loved ones, their thoughts heavily shrouded by the memory of recent traumatic events.

Hundreds of these small tents had been erected in straight rows, covering the sprawling grounds behind an old government school building. The light from the candles or kerosene lamps in the tents, though poorly illuminating the interior, attracted swarms of flying insects outside. These feeble lights were no match to the enveloping darkness of the moonless night outside.

*

Six-year-old Daman lay under the vastness of that sky, in the dark outside his tent. His father, Charan, had preferred to stay inside, but his grandfather, Daji, was with him. Daji had decided to bring Daman out in the open to divert his fragile young mind.

"Do we all turn into stars after we die?" Daman asked in a timid voice.

Daji had his right arm under Daman's head to provide him comfort of constant contact and protection against the roughness of the hard grass under them. He wanted to keep Daman as close to him as possible.

"Yes, we do, and then we shine for ever," said Daji reassuringly, looking up at the sky.

"Where is Ma then?" Daman asked, searching Daji's face for the solemn signs that would reassure him of the authenticity of his grandfather's response.

The fragile lightness of Daman's body against his reminded Daji of the gravity of the impact of premature maternal bereavement on him. In order to provide an instant consoling response, Daji's eyes sought out Arcturus, the most prominent star in the vastness of the sky, and pointed to it.

"Why is my Ma's star so lonely in that big sky?" asked Daman immediately, staring at the star.

"No Daman, that is not true, when we look at somebody we love so intimately, we do not notice things around them."

Daji looked into Daman's eyes to check for signs of doubt. Reassured, he continued, "There are many other stars close to your Ma but your eyes will fail to notice them, because you love your Ma so much. Is that not true? We will all join her one day, in that sky, forming new stars around her and then we all will be together again, for ever."

"Is Maun also there with her?" asked the boy, thinking about his dog. A few tears dripped from Daman's eyes, wetting his grandfather's arm.

Daji's eyes also became wet. He held Daman's forehead, kissing it gently.

The sharp whistle of a train as it passed by broke their soft embrace and produced a sudden shudder in their bodies. The rattling sound and the vibration of the ground created by the passing train shook the entire camp.

The small railway station of Dahota was only few hundred yards away from their camp and was on a railway line which connected several Indian states with the north. Though many trains, both goods and passenger, passed through this station, only a few of them stopped. With the ongoing massive human movement across the newly declared borders, many new trains were now running on these routes. They carried many to the new homes prescribed by their beloved leaders on the basis of their religion, whether they wished to move or not.

The sound of the passing train triggered Daji's memories of their old home, now in the new nation of Pakistan, and also their escape on the train that had deposited them in this refugee camp.

"Daji why did our train take so long to whistle?" Daman asked him now.

Daji kept silent, as if searching the depths of his own mind for an answer. The memories of their recent escape and the human betrayals were still fresh.

His mind replayed the tragedy of their journey.

*

They had been lucky to evade the prying eyes of the lynching mobs to get to the railway station under the darkness of night. The charred remnants of orgiastic destruction surrounded them. Their long-time housemaid, Farida, had been insistent on accompanying them to the station. Her requests were firmly denied by Charan, as they did not wish to endanger her life as well.

Maun, their four-year-old dog, had silently followed them through the familiar lanes and byways of what had once been their own town, now littered with burnt and broken remnants of the day's orgy. It was very unusual behaviour for Maun, who, contrary to his name, was always noisy. It seemed as if he had a premonition of the coming separation. Just a day before, his animated barks of dismay and alarm had been contemptuously disregarded by the mob that looted their house without any fear. During this attack, the family had stayed hidden in the attic, among their household discards.

After reaching the railway station it was not difficult to spot their intended train. Maun was in no mood to say goodbye and followed them right up to the train. As they struggled to gain access to the crowded train, Maun stood by, wagging his tail and softly barking to remind them of his presence.

While they squeezed their way into the compartment, Maun had become more and more restless and agitated as the reality of a permanent separation slowly dawned upon him. Daman's pleas to not leave Maun behind fell on deaf ears. Once all the family was in, a bewildered passenger, seemingly worried that they might change their mind and bring the dog in, slammed the door shut.

That was the unceremonious adieu to their beloved dog. Maun, by virtue of being a creature with no religious belief, was not a target of the current frenzy and therefore could safely stay back in this new religious state.

*

The train, which was destined to take them across newly man-made borders, stood stationary for hours without any signs of movement. There were no lights in their compartment and all the windows and doors had been securely shut.

Intermittently, there had been hysterical hammering on the doors and windows, most likely by desperate people trying to gain access to their only hope of an escape. All these knocks were perceived as potential threats and received with a concerted cry of "Do not open."

In this dark, congested train compartment, the sounds of laboured and anxious breathing were interspersed with either a cry of despair or the sudden unfolding of surging fears. The meagre reserve of oxygen in that enclosed compartment was being quickly consumed, leaving only fetid air laced with evaporated sweat. This added to the fear and severe claustrophobia being experienced by the desperate occupants.

To make matters worse, the distant pulsating whirr of a slogan-shouting mob, slowly inching closer, could be heard. The echo of the voices raised in unison by the self-appointed brutal enforcers and cleansing strategists was frequently punctuated by a burst of the metallic rattle of swords, fire explosions and heart-rending shrieks. The growing closeness of this noise added to the atmosphere of profound fear within. The rhythmic sounds of the recitation of prayers to the Almighty soon filled the train compartment.

Charan had been able to secure the seat next to the window for his wife Bani and his father Daji, who held Daman in his lap. Charan himself chose to stand sandwiched among the heaving mass of mortals a few yards away from his family.

Bani was six months pregnant and the company of an elderly person and a young child had got them the prime window seat. Daji held Daman in his lap with a firm grip lightly covering him with his light grey pashmina shawl. Bani sat in a tight corner with her feet drawn over the berth so as to provide sufficient room for another lady to sit on the floor beneath her seat. The presence of his mother next to him and the closeness of his beloved Daji gave Daman a sense of being completely protected. His right hand softly held the left ankle of his mother, which provided a great source of solace for him.

Daman's repeated question, "When will this train move?" had been answered each time by his grandfather with a single monotonous syllable, "Soon."

Not only Daman, but all the other passengers also waited anxiously for signs of the train's movement.

*

Bani thought about her deserted house and the belongings she had been unable to salvage. She thought disconsolately about the photo albums, containing photographs from her marriage and other ceremonies and functions they had in happier times. She also thought of the many gifts given to her or to Daman by her parents and other relatives on birthdays or festivals. She recalled how, during their escape from home, a crying Daman had to be virtually dragged away from his beloved bicycle, which he held on to vehemently, not understanding the gravity of their flight.

Bani had been able to pick up her precious jewellery, which was divided between three adults for safety. Her hand inadvertently touched the top of her kameez to get the reassuring feel of a small bundle of gold bangles stashed under her bra.

There was a sudden jolt, a loud thud, and a sharp train whistle, announcing its departure. This shook Bani out of her pensive stance. This was the first ever sign of the presence of an active engine capable of steaming out with its load of despondent passengers.

This sign of motion resulted in the sudden activation of ominous sounds of an approaching mob, which so far had sounded only like a distant bedlam. The frantic knocking on doors and windows had now clearly turned into sounds of attempts to break in. The agitated and roused imprecations, "Do not let the kafirs go! They have massacred a train full of Muslims in Ferozepur!" gave a clear sign of their intentions.

Bani's breathing was slowly becoming deeper. She was developing a deep sinking sensation in her stomach, reminiscent of her morning sickness. Suddenly she descended into a panic attack, holding with difficulty onto a mouthful of her stomach contents, brought up by both her pregnancy and fear.

The train had now started to move slowly, and this was accompanied by increasing sounds of chasing footsteps outside.

Bani could not hold in her mouthful of vomit and in an attempt to avoid spewing it over the lady sitting beneath her, she attempted to raise her window. Everyone in the compartment accosted her with a stern warning, but the harm had already been done. Suddenly a pair of dark hands with rough and stained fingers thrust into the slit created by Bani's attempt to open the window.

Her further endeavour to thrust the steel frame of the window down proved futile against the brute force of a determined man. Another pair of hands appeared soon after, adding strength to his resolve. The resisting force provided by Daji and a few others was proving futile.

The slowly increasing speed and sounds of the train added to the deafening clamour of slogan-shouting and the hysterical activities on the platform. The window was forced open from outside, confirmed by the sudden entry of light and a whiff of fresh air. The choleric faces of at least two persons with scornful grins and unsightly, stained teeth were now clearly distinguishable. The expressions of contempt and rage on their faces paralysed the people inside with fear.

Running alongside the slow-moving train, they had caught hold of Bani's arms and hair, and were trying to drag her out of the window. There were the constant cries of the accompanying mob, "Do not let go of the bitch!" Their brutal grip on their prey kept on pulling Bani out of the window, which had no restraints. In a swift movement one of them grabbed her right breast and the feel of a small metallic bundle added strength to his grip, increased by the prospect of additional loot.

"This bitch is carrying gold out of our land, while our brethren are being butchered in India," he shouted, his voice remorseless.

The tug of war between two sides, in and out of the train, was interspersed with hysterical cries of many, including Daji and Charan. Daman's grip on his mother's left ankle was now stronger than ever. They seemed to be losing this tussle, as more and more of Bani's body was being pulled out through the window. Bani's frantic cries for help were lost in the din of the slogan-shouting mob on the platform.

The train had now gained speed and so did the flapping sounds from slippers worn by those on the platform as they tried harder to hang on. Bani slowly gave up her resistance, her mind paralysed by fear and her lean body being pulled like a mass of lifeless flesh. Suddenly there was a big thud; her body had hit a signal post. Her dress and hair tangled with the metallic frame of the post; her body was twisted and pulled outwards. The train continued on its way while she was pulled out of the window, slowly escaping the last gentle grip of Daman's small hands.

It was over in fraction of a minute; all that remained inside were her slippers on the seat and the soft, quiet sobs of Daji, Daman, Charan and others.

The space created by her sudden disappearance remained unoccupied for the rest of the journey and her slippers adorned it, creating a small shrine. A grim silence prevailed.

*

Daji's thoughts were suddenly disrupted by a commotion outside the tents close to the cluster of trees. He raised his head from the ground to look at Daman and also to get a better glimpse of the uproar. A few people had rushed out of their tents and were looking around with the help of feeble torchlights.

Daji picked Daman up and joined the group of onlookers, which had swollen to more than a dozen now. There was an increase in their agitated movements, followed by sudden chasing and shouts of "Snake, snake!"

A snake had unfortunately found its way into one of the tents and had woken up the inhabitant by its frighteningly smooth crawl touching his foot. The alarmed man jumped out of his bed, throwing the snake onto the floor. It was a rough-scaled snake with a slender body and a brownish zigzag pattern on his back. He had screamed in fear, "Oh God, it could have sucked away my breath." His cry was based on an old fear of paralysis.

After an initial struggle to find an escape route, the snake had managed to squirm its way into a collection of stones just outside the tent. Its tail continued to wriggle and lay bare, in clear view of the terrified onlookers who stood at a safe distance, debating its species, with almost all agreeing it must be a poisonous one.

For them, all snakes meant death and terror and therefore did not deserve to be left alive, though few had the courage to take the lead in killing.

Perhaps their state of paranoia compelled them to suspect any alien species as dangerous. Some of them by now had found strong sticks and with a reluctant push, tried to dislodge the stones.

A person standing some distance away reminded the stick-bearers about snakes being revengeful, and the possibility of either it or its mate (if it was killed) returning to take revenge.

A second suggestion soon followed, issuing a warning to any pregnant female to not look at the snake, as she could lose her eyesight. Fortunately, no pregnant woman was around.

The first attempt to hit the snake was immediately greeted with the remark, "No use hitting the tail, it will grow back again." Then somebody made a moral observation, reminding the striker about the sin he would commit if he killed the snake. No thought was spared for the right of that creature to live and ironically even its killing was considered a taboo only because there was the risk of carrying sin.

The snake was becoming a victim not because it had done any harm, but due to its race and appearance, which was similar to a few poisonous species. No thought was given to the fact that creature had not harmed anyone and was in the process of going about his natural routine activities of finding food.

*

A short and burly Sikh in his mid-forties, with a moustache and long dark loose beard, had so far been a silent spectator. He was dressed in his shorts, baring his strong hairy legs. A short blue turban, wet on his forehead from sweat, covered his head.

He suddenly shoved aside the people in front. Lurching forward, he snatched the stick out of the hand of a person standing in front, and pushed aside the stones covering the snake. This bared almost half of the body of the snake, trying its best to coil its way into the remaining gaps, in a last attempt at escape. The man was in no mood for mercy, fresh from his latest experience in dealing with threats.

He started to hit the snake in a repeated assault on the middle of its back. The snake coiled back with alarming speed, attempting to protect its wounded back and to create fear in his assailant. This did produce a wave of fright among the onlookers, and a collective "Oh…" was heard from them as they stepped back. But the attacker did not, for he had found the perfect target now to hit at, the snake's head.

It took another few solid hits on its head for this living creature to turn into a lifeless lump of flesh. The man lifted the dead snake like a trophy on his stick, handing it back into the trembling hands of the man from whom he had taken it.

"Go and bury this somewhere, so that a dog may not eat it, that can make him rabid," he commanded, and disappeared through the crowd towards his tent.

Daman remained a silent spectator to all this drama, and tis silence continued till they were back on the ground where they had been lying down before.

"Why did they kill that snake? Was she also a kafir?" Daman asked in a muffled voice.

Daji had nothing to say for a while. He pondered over the depth of Daman's question. Was there any sensible explanation for all the killings going on? Why someone who does not have the same ideology, way of life, or appearance becomes a kafir?

He looked into Daman's eyes and said, "Some bad people invent ways to hate and kill. For them anybody who does not listen to them or live like them is a 'kafir'. Many are not like that. Farida was not like that."

"Oh, yes..." Daman said, his eyes getting heavy with sleep, but he did not want to shut his eyes and lose the sight of his Ma star. With the vision of the Ma star still before his eyes, he finally fell asleep. Daji picked him up and took him inside the tent. His eyes misted over, wondering whether Daman would learn to live with love and not hatred in his heart.

* * *

Living in Afterlife

The ear-piercing sound of shattering glass, followed by the sudden intrusion of sneaky rays of sunlight that crawled all over the floor of my dark room made my heart miss a beat. That sound and light broke the sanctity of my solitude. Slowly, my quickened heartbeats returned to normal. As I calmed down, I managed a faint smile, for I had heard sounds of young feet running past and fading away. I slowly got up from the bed and forced myself to put a patch over the cracked glass, to restore my solitude.

*

Since the age of sixty-eight, I had been living alone in this one-room dwelling. When I turned eighty, I had a strange dream in which I was half-suspended in air, levitating, defying the laws of gravity. The envious stares of my friends and near and dear ones told me that I was in a coveted position. They leaped repeatedly to get me down, but I was beyond their reach. Obviously, they envied my sublime suspension. When I opened my eyes, I told myself that the dream had a clear message for me. It was time to start the transition towards my inevitable afterlife.

I wanted to do it in style.

*

My obsession with the idea soon caught up with me as my brain started to get flooded with ideas about my afterlife, flush with objects of my desire. I dreamed of a silk-lined, well-equipped sarcophagus, or rather a tomb, packed with things dear to me. It would be a Pharaoh's envy, of course, complete with a decorated overhead stone sign screaming "Living in Afterlife".

I was getting super-excited and also a tad nervous, but I was definitely in control, as I started my preparations with a list of do's and don'ts for my transfer from this modest earthly abode to the abode of angels. More and more ideas poured in every day to my excited brain, getting me increasingly stirred.

To reach Pharaoh-like dimensions, my afterlife wish-list soon expanded like a balloon: my favourite bed, silk sheets, favourite wine on the bedside, the books I loved, white roses…the list was endless. The balloon of my wishes never burst and I was in the clouds, ready to invest all my savings in this. After all, my current abode was not going to exist for long.

I found a shabti in an old antique shop. In an ethereal blue shade, arms folded in front, her dignified pose held a sign of sublime surrender and humility in death. She quickly became my inspiration and an eternal companion.

I had to transform myself to attain those very qualities of immensity and humility. To achieve this, I performed mock drills in my small room. With all doors and windows closed, curtains drawn, wearing my black suit and white shirt with a black bow, lying flat on my back arms crossed over my chest, I wandered off into a corpse-like posture with shabti at my side. I succeeded in erasing my current life attachments from my mind and to lose myself in this new world. Amazingly, my claustrophobic mind didn't detest it. With gravity gone, I levitated. I heard nothing. The sound waves froze around me as universal physical laws ceased to exist.

My excitement grew further as I furthered my acceptance of solitary confinement. I was falling in love with my self-imposed internment, drowning in a dream-like state. A mix of many dreams joined together to give a collective meaning to my blissful new afterlife.

An apparition – a daemonic incarnation, my intrusive self, did visit me during those stances, attempting to dissuade me. I wanted to raise my hand to push it away, but dead hands don't move, so I resisted the urge. I smiled, feeling victorious as I saw my present fizzling away. Newton's forces were failing as my body levitated higher and higher. I felt ecstatic about my detached status. I was ready.

The time had come for me to execute those ideas and to make arrangements for this dignified (after) lifestyle.

*

I was in a hurry and soon found an instant cash funeral deal from the web. It seemed suitable, promising afterlife arrangements according to the client's wish. I promptly contacted that person who assured me that he could arrange everything I asked for; in fact, he seemed very enthusiastic. He agreed to provide a special stone sarcophagus in my desired design, with the silk lining, shabti on my chest and all the items on my list enclosed and by my side. And, yes, also a stone over it with the inscription, "Living in Afterlife".

My excitement was running high. Happily, I handed over the cash and sealed the deal. Reassured of my dream coming true I started living parallel lives – mostly imitating my afterlife, alone in a dark room pretending to be dead, with my current life taking a back seat. I waited anxiously to be in my sarcophagus. Everything seemed to be in place.

*

Weeks passed by. My memory of those stone-throwers was fading fast and the tape securing the smashed window went unnoticed. My near and dear ones tried futilely to interfere, but they failed to derail my pursuit. For once being alone and a widower was proving to be a blessing.

Then came a shock in the form of a poorly written note slipped under my door: *"Penniless, facing an early death from cancer, I cheated you through your funeral plan. This was the only way I could fulfil my desire to go for my pilgrimage before death. I don't have much time left now and hope you will pardon me. Wishing you a peaceful life!"*

Everything around me came crashing down – my dreams, my half-lost self. Much like the broken windowpane, my desires for a great afterlife were shattered. Picking up the pieces of what was left, I was forced to reinvent my present life.

Surprisingly it didn't take long to change my plan from peaceful afterlife to peaceful life. I didn't have a choice anyway. My faithful shabti in all her grace still lies by my side, arms still folded in submission, her blue vastness still inviting, her divine sanctity promising an unending companionship, her magnanimity reassuring in its promise to stay with me through my journey in this life.

* * *

An Angel Warrior

It was a small Cessna aircraft with six passengers, including our family of three, a couple – most likely Highlanders – and their piglet. Our fellow passengers' origin was not hard to guess from their attire and of course the destination – Goroka, a small town in the Highlands of Papua New Guinea. Yes, there was a small piglet accompanying them, affectionately wrapped in a hand-woven, multicoloured woollen jacket with a rope around its neck to keep control in case of a need. He sat just beside me, a bit restless in that claustrophobic enclosure. He had sniffed me furiously as soon as I took my seat, and fortunately approved my presence. The young pilot, possibly used to having such customers on board, still kept an eye on him to monitor his potential for creating an unexpected porcine disruption.

My five-year-old daughter Hina sat in a row behind me with her mother, a bit worried about the piglet, but mostly fascinated by the view out of the small window next to her. She also regularly stole a glance at the piglet. The sight of the vast green forest canopy under us was simply breathtaking.

We were flying from Lae, a coastal town, to the Highlands. As we entered the Highland region, strong winds welcomed us, making our aircraft shudder. It shook like a dry leaf, frightening all, particularly the Highlander couple. Agitated, the pig also made low guttural sounds of protest.

Hina looked worried; my wife, Neena, frowned with fear. The pilot, unconcerned, continued to hum a local tune, obviously familiar with these upheavals. He never felt a need to make a formal announcement about the turbulence.

I looked out of the small window next to me again. The green hillside was now becoming interspersed with tin roofs or thatched huts with streaks of smoke snaking out. Their number started to increase gradually and then few dirt pathways joining them could also be seen. Soon these pathways grew into a partially metalled road indicating an approaching larger human habitation.

Finally, to our relief, the first ever announcement came – about the approaching Goroka airport. There were sighs of relief. The faces of the Highlander couple were illuminated by escalating joy and the delight of homecoming. Their piglet sat frozen, seemingly terrified by the sudden loss of height.

The plane had taken a sharp nose-down and headed for what looked like a poorly metalled runway. The moment its wheels touched the ground a cloud of dust arose, enveloping the plane. It shook violently, making the pig squeal. All of us gripped our hand rests, while Hina's fingers reached for her mother's hand.

The plane continued its run out of the cloud of dust towards a small building, the Goroka Airport terminal. There was a fence separating the runway from a town road which ran parallel to it. On the other side of fence stood many locals, curiously looking at the arriving plane. Young ladies, some holding kids, stood watching, mostly wearing local attire, many with fanciful head dresses. Some had colourful bilums hung over their heads.

Soon we were ushered into a bag-claiming area: a tin shed with many onlookers, way outnumbering the arriving passengers. My wife's face held a look of disappointment. Perhaps she was expecting at least some semblance of

Western civilisation. A huge colourful billboard showing a bird of paradise stared down, reading "Welcome to the Land of the Unexpected."

Hina was frightened, being surrounded by locals in their traditional attire, some carrying bush knives while a few others carried bows and arrows. She held my hand in a tight squeeze. Her main focus soon turned to a short-statured man, older than others, in a grass skirt with a bunch of leaves tucked into the back with a woven strip in the front, intently staring at her. He wore a headdress made of multicoloured feathers, though the jewel in his crown was a turquoise plume made from a bird-of-paradise tail embedded into cuscus fur. He had a big butterfly tattoo on his forehead. His nose was pierced by a curved bone, which I later learned was a pig tusk. He had a necklace made out of white seashells, bright wild seeds and bone pieces adorning his neck. These were supposed to ward off bush spirits. He held a bow and arrows, and a bush knife was tucked securely into his waist. Like most of the mob surrounding us, he wore no footwear.

The old man continued to look at Hina as he made his way through the crowd to approach her. His earthy body odour smelled of nature, as did his attire. He gave a broad smile, revealing betel-nut stained teeth. His dull eyes appeared to me devoid of both worldly greed and fear. However, Hina was terrified. Realising this, he plucked a colourful feather out of his crown and offered it to her. She accepted it reluctantly. And then he just melted away in the crowd.

A voice soon called my name. This was Joe, my local contact, who had come to collect us.

"Welcome to the Land of Unexpected," he said, and I couldn't agree more. He came forward, we shook hands and he quickly started to help me with my bags, putting them in his pickup van. With formal introductions and a formal chitchat, "No problem with your flight?", "It was okay?" etc. he cleared us through the crowd, helped by loud instructions in a local dialect.

"Oh," he said, "I noticed an old man in sing-sing attire approaching you. Don't worry. He's just a strange man – a regular at the airport whenever a flight comes in. He means no harm; his name is Tomas and he lives nearby in a small village up that hill," Joe said, pointing towards a hill to the west of Goroka. Joe continued, "He lost his son and a four-year-old granddaughter in an air crash a few years ago. His own people told him the plane just ran out of fuel and fell down. Ever since then he roams the town streets, as if searching for his lost loved ones."

We soon reached our destination – our new abode, which was situated right on the town's main road. It was an old weatherboard house surrounded by huge tracts of open land and many trees. We didn't have much energy to explore further and decided to retire early that evening. My jet-lagged sleep extended well into the next day only to be interrupted by a hullaballoo on the town road just outside our front fence. I looked at my watch; it was already half-past ten in the morning.

The commotion was getting louder with many voices screaming and laughing in unison. I rushed to the window to have a better look. A crowd had gathered on the roadside and there seemed to be an obstruction to the traffic flow, with vehicles stalled on both sides. Among the crowd I could distinctly see a turquoise bird-of-paradise plume, possibly the centre of that commotion, moving around.

My curiosity piqued, I quickly put on a gown and walked out.

I was not wrong. It was Tomas at the epicentre of that commotion. Strangely, he was repetitively crossing a pedestrian zebra crossing, backward and forwards, halting vehicular traffic on both sides as the crowd cheered him on and the car drivers yelled. I smiled, for Tomas had discovered the power of being on that newly introduced pedestrian crossing, halting the traffic on both sides. He was enjoying it to his fullest. As he crossed this time to come face-to-face with me, he stopped.

I had no idea why my family or I would fascinate him so much. Our eyes met. I smiled, but he didn't. He just seemed to be intrigued by me. I came back home with a gut feeling that we hadn't seen the last of Tomas.

*

Next day when I came home for lunch, Tomas was sitting just next to our front door. I went in to find that both Neena and Hina, terrified, had shut themselves inside. They told me about their visit to the town for some grocery shopping and how Tomas followed them closely and walked back to the house with them. I smiled, held Hina's hand and pulled her out with me to confront Tomas.

"Api-noon," I greeted him, using the few words of greeting I had learned. This time he did smile, extending his hand to touch Hina's head, but she moved back. I pulled two kina coins out of my pocket and offered them to him. He simply refused. I thought of another way of paying for his escort job and asked Hina to get a one-litre carton of milk they had just bought. I handed that over to Tomas. He not only accepted it, but drank it straight away.

I thought that would settle the cost of his unbidden escort services. Satisfied, we went inside and later I returned to my workplace. By evening I had all but forgotten about Tomas. As we all sat around a table for dinner, I was alarmed by what sounded like a cough, and the crackling sounds of burning wood in my back yard. I looked through the window. Tomas had lit a small fire and was sitting next to it, with his bow and arrows close by his side. It was now clear that he had taken full charge as our self-appointed security. I went out and handed him a plate of food we had cooked. He accepted that graciously.

Next day I confronted Tomas again. His response was either nothing, or just a wide smile. However, the unspoken message was crystal clear: "I am not leaving soon." I had no other option but to formalise his appointment. I showed him a small hut I had in my backyard, built with kunai grass, with a fire pit in the middle. He loved it and soon made that his home. Days and nights went by. He would disappear every day in the morning for few hours and then come back in the evening, before sunset, carrying a load of dry wood for his night-time fire. It also didn't take long before he became addicted to our rice and curry meals, which we shared with him every evening.

Hina had also, by now, lost her fear of him and loved to peep into his "liklik haus" (small house), as he affectionately called it.

*

One day he brought a small black puppy and we named it Pugsy. Hina loved playing with Pugsy under the watchful eyes of Tomas. He would also occasionally play a strange, flute-like musical instrument made from a split bamboo with a piece of string attached at one end.

More days passed by. Tomas brought many gifts for us, especially for Hina, ranging from carved wooden masks to a ritual wooden axe, its handle strapped with dried grass shoots.

He never accepted money, only rice and curry, which became his daily dinner.

One day, Pugsy, now a mature seven months old, went missing. Tomas was worried. "He is juicy. We must find him soon," he said, scared that being well fed, Pugsy may be lured away by somebody for feasting. He spent the next three days in the search, coming home later than usual in the evening. Luckily, Pugsy reappeared on the third night, muddy and dirty. He quietly snuggled into Tomas's side as he slept next to the pit fire in his home.

During these three days I had seen sadness in his eyes, but never a streak of fear. I was learning this novel human behaviour from the ones so close to nature. Fear of other humans, a key to most worldly actions or inactions, deeds or misdeeds, was not the driving force behind our Angel Warrior's persona. He had no fear of the law or even the knowledge of one. His existence was close to nature. He didn't seem to have a recognisable god. Perhaps he never needed one. However, the tribal way of life did teach him about certain threats, mostly from supernatural evil spirits. He also knew the ways to ward these off.

His attachment to Hina and our household was not definable either; perhaps he saw in me and Hina his lost son and granddaughter. Even then this bonding remained undefined. However great the cultural differences between us, he had somehow succeeded in interweaving his prevailing emotions into this relationship. He never showed these emotions on his face. I never saw him crying or even laughing. He had no multi-layered mask on his face like most of us, just a wooden face, designed by nature, quite resembling the mask he made and gifted us. My first impression of him never changed over months.

As time flew by and our departure came near, Tomas, by some sixth sense, became more and more concerned about Hina. He had now stopped going away during the day and instead started going daily to Hina's school. He waited outside until she had finished her school and I picked her up.

Then the day came for our departure. We were all packed to leave. My eyes searched Tomas' face. He was restless but again without any signs of fear. He had spent the last few days making a small doll with bamboo strips and kunai grass which he kept in his "liklik haus". On the day of our departure, for first time, I hugged him. My eyes were wet but his were not. I saw just blankness in them. He went to Hina and sat in front of her with Pugsy behind him, and presented her with the grass doll. Deeply touched, Hina accepted the doll, and looked at me, as if asking, "Papa, can't Tomas come with us?" I offered him a wad of kina notes as a parting gift which he refused.

Joe drove us to the airport. We were all quiet as if scared of breaking down as soon as one of us spoke a word. Once we boarded, Hina sat with me as I looked out of the window. My eyes searched for Tomas and Pugsy.

The plane started its run and my eyes were focused across the fence, desperately searching for what I was leaving behind. I knew he would be there. As the plane raced forward, I finally saw Tomas, a canister in hand, running along the fence. He was desperately trying to reach out, with panting Pugsy in tow. He was gesticulating frantically, as if soulfully crying out "Brada plis take extra bensin (gasoline), your balus (aeroplane) may run short."

As we flew away, his image got smaller and smaller, ultimately turning into a speck in that vast landscape we were leaving behind. A speck that he always was.

* * *

Mirroring a Smile

It was like any other day. The slowly rising melody of morning street sounds, birds singing, the sound of rustling leaves, had the same old tenor. The dawning light got on with its business of eliminating the darkness in our small room, its evolving shades changing by the minute. Split as it went through a crack in the old window glass, it formed an imperfect rainbow on the facing wall, a distinct albeit distorted image of a lingering hope, shimmering nervously.

A lava lamp on a corner table released a continuous array of different-sized bubbles, persistently craving attention. The moment they were born, big or small, they rushed to reach the top, as if competing with each other. A rag doll, in her dull striped frock, sat quietly on the bedside table. She seemed to be waiting endlessly, staring into an abyss, the smile on her clown face almost gone.

These three things: the lava lamp, the rag doll, and the shadows on the wall were the first things Misha's eyes looked for as soon as they opened in the morning.

*

Hidden behind the doll was a three-year old family photograph of three smiling faces, either spontaneous or insisted upon by one who may be called a perfectionist photographer. My wife, who treasured her smile most, left soon after, hurrying past us to reach the pleasures she always sought. She was very much like the winning lava lamp bubble right at the top, while Misha and I remained at the bottom, unnoticed.

My wife's parting gift, that photograph with the unfaded smile of togetherness frozen in time, remained with us, as if preserved in a time capsule. Misha had ever since been fascinated by the shadows on the wall and the lava lamp bubbles, as if searching for her mother in them.

The brazen light, finally triumphant over the darkness in our room, shone over Misha's eyes. This wake-up call never failed. As her eyes opened, she looked at the lava lamp, the rag doll, the shadows on the wall. Then she looked for me, to be reassured of my presence.

Her penetrating eyes, the most versatile and visible part of her face, searched my expressions. Her face, partly weakened by cerebral palsy, remained emotionless and devoid of a happy expression, especially since her mother's departure. It was as if her facial muscles had gone into in a deep slumber. I had, over the last three years, done my best to get her smile back with fun parks and gifts, but nothing had worked and I felt defeated.

All we could do now was to search each other's face for that elusive happiness.

Lost in my thoughts, feeling dejected, I turned away from my daughter. I stopped and stood in front of a nearby mirror and searched my face. A grim image stared back at me, eerily resembling Misha's face.

"Can I change my expression?" I wondered, and attempted to bring a smile on my face. I realised how far away I was from happiness and was not sure whether I could bring myself to it. I tried again but my eyes continued to reflect sadness. My gaze dropped further and the image still looked dejected.

A string of thoughts flashed through my mind.

My image is a slave to my thoughts.

Are Misha's expressions, just like my own, slaves to what she observes on my face?

Am I a mirror image for Misha?

Can I change my thoughts and bring a smile on my face?

Will a smile on my face bring her smile back?

A spark appeared in my eyes like a ray of hope ready to sweep through my body, like that small bubble in the lava lamp left behind by the winners, now learning to compete. My determination grew steadily, as did the stream of those gratifying thoughts. A faint smile slowly appeared on my face. Feeling excited now, I turned back to look at Misha. Her expression changed instantaneously. She looked amazed.

This magnified my smile further. Misha's facial muscles responded, showing a sequence of small twitches. An innocent smile seemed to be appearing on her face. It was working; Misha's face was copying my expression.

I prayed, "Oh God, please don't stop this!"

Her emerging smile started to look similar to the rainbow on the wall – shimmering, faint, yet with colours of hope. Her smile was becoming bigger and brighter like the light in the room. As it became deeper it started to reach her lips, her eyes and then spread all over her face. Every single muscle on her face now smiled and seemed to be celebrating.

Everything in the room began reverberating with that happiness. The doll's smile came back, the bubbles in the lava lamp now rose in unison and the shadows on the wall danced in celebration.

Then she had her first ever giggle.

I reciprocated, giggling with her. Her face illuminated. I bent over and kissed her.

Her hands reached out for the doll.

* * *

Ravana's Third Rib

It was *Basant Panchami* – a day to welcome the spring season in northern India. The kite fliers occupied most of the rooftops in and around our town. Dressed in their colourful best, they cheered as their well-crafted kites outdid others. Each flier's dextrous fingers skilfully controlled a kite with the help of a devoted helper holding the string roll, standing by his side.

Tastefully designed and decorated kites flew everywhere. Flying majestically, they became the objects of envy for the heights they scaled or their artful diving skills. Some, though not reaching great heights, made their mark with their bird or butterfly shapes or their long, fluttering paper ribbon tails. They shimmered, flapped and floated proudly in the clear sky helped by gentle February winds.

Success in this craft of kite flying depended on relentless training, skilful designing and the use of reinforced strings. It required a great deal to ensure a win. The win in this game was success in hacking the contender's kite.

"*Woh Kataa---*" – a winner's war cry suddenly penetrated the surroundings. Somebody had successfully eliminated his contender's kite after a long, torrid sky battle. As the victory call resonated in the lanes and byways of our small dusty town, dozens of boys, the looters in waiting, got into action. A limp, powerless kite swaying aimlessly in the sky was their prey. As the hunters keenly watched its fall, their bodies, pumping adrenaline, sprang into action.

I was one of them, eleven years old and dressed in my spring best.

The centre of action had now descended from the rooftops to our pumped-up group of contenders.

The moment the bugle declaring the ground battle blared, the unfortunate owner of the hacked kite was swiftly forgotten. His kite was no man's property now.

Looting a loose kite was not a simple task but required practice, experience and fitness. The looters, aged between six and fifteen years, were ready to become ferocious competitors.

All eyes were now fixed on the trophy – the defeated kite. It was a bright blue one with big yellow circles on its wings. As it swayed helplessly, at the mercy of the wind, we observed its direction and calculated the location of its eventual fall onto the ground.

The obstacle race then commenced, with fences and drains to be jumped, and other runners to be pushed away mercilessly.

The sounds of dozens of running feet and cries of "Lootoh! – grab!" alarmed the street dogs who ran helter-skelter. The residents in the houses lining these lanes rushed out, either to enjoy the spectacle or worried about their gardens and property.

I was a good runner and an experienced hand in looting, as were a few others. Slowly the leaders of the race started to emerge and very soon it was just two of us at the front. The boy competing with me was of a similar age and build.

We ran ferociously. As the kite came within our reach, both of us jumped to claim it and simultaneously put our hands on it. Trying not to pull it too hard, lest we rip it, we became joint claimants of the coveted trophy.

As we held on to the kite and looked at each other, I realised his grip was firmer than mine. He simply ignored my presence and waited for me to let go. My eyes scanned him; we were of similar heights, but he had fairer skin, sharp features and thick dark black hair which was heavily oiled. He wore khaki shorts and a partially open off-white shirt with few missing buttons. There was a cloth bag slung over his right shoulder. He seemed to be from a poor family.

What struck me most were his dark penetrating eyes prominently outlined with black surma. He stared at me, giving me a threatening look. The message was clear: "Don't mess with me." Mesmerised, I let go my grip on the kite, and he claimed victory.

He took a step back, pulled a small red comb out of his back pocket and started to reset his hair triumphantly. He was combing his dishevelled tuft as if readjusting a bedraggled crown.

We stood facing, weighing each other up. I had no intention of engaging in a fight.

I looked at his feet. He was wearing ill-fitting rubber sandals; I wore a pair of sports shoes. I instantly realised that he had competed with a handicap and won.

I smiled at him and extended my hand of friendship, which he accepted reluctantly. His initial hesitation though was only momentary.

"I am Vasu. What is your name?" he said, suddenly opening up.

After a short and formal exchange, his unstoppable rhetoric started, about him and his skill of kite looting. He told me he had a big collection of looted kites and that one day he would open a kite shop.

Eager to strengthen our friendship further, he wanted me to know more about him.

"Come, I will show you something," he said, as he wrapped the kite's string onto his left hand.

It didn't take long for me to become inconsequential. From then on it was all about Vasu, by Vasu and for Vasu.

*

He dragged me to a big peepal tree which stood near the outskirts of our city. As we entered its massive canopy, he plucked a leaf from a low-lying branch. He reverently touched it on to his forehead, bowed low and ordered me to bow as well.

The peepal tree's huge trunk had vermilion threads tied around it. There was a brick layered platform built around its trunk, on which lay a few flowers – offerings by devotees.

Vasu then proceeded towards a rock that lay just behind the tree. It was about five to six feet high, and he climbed it from its rear. After some effort he made himself comfortable on its slippery surface. The trophy kite steadfastly remained with him, well secured in his left hand.

Under the dark shadow of that tree there were many snake-like aerial roots hanging down. They swayed mysteriously around me with the wind. There also had been tales of a ghost living on that tree. I began to panic, but tried to hide it.

Vasu sat on the rock majestically, watching me, sensing my discomfort and gloating over it.

He spoke as if he was addressing his subject- "My grandmother once told me that I could talk to my *Kul-Devta* (family deity) from this spot."

"That day came soon after. My Kul-Devta spoke to me right here and told me about my impending Raj Yoga – my period of prosperity."

He looked up, closed his eyes and bowed his head in devotion. Then he folded the leaf he carried, put it against his lips and started to play music with it.

He stopped for a moment and asked "Do you like my peepli music? This is how I bond with my Kul-Devta. These notes of music help me fill the void created between me and my Kul-Devta by the noises of you mortals." He started playing the peepli music again.

I realised the notes he produced were all based on bird sounds, some mimicking the calls of a koel. I was impressed. He must have learned these sounds by his day-to-day observations of the bird life around him.

"I invented this music," said Vasu, pleased with the admiration evident on my face. He continued his talk, trying to overwhelm me with his personality and the amazing skills he believed he had. I must admit, I had by now become extremely curious.

Vasu constantly talked and I listened, almost hypnotised. He had found a good listener and I had found a good storyteller. He bombarded me with further stories about himself, making sure I had no opportunity to break out of his spell.

*

Vasu then led me to a path that ran parallel to a railway track. He continued to talk, mostly about his family's glory, lost in the Partition of 1947. His talks were interrupted occasionally when he stopped to pick up pieces of coal that had fallen from running trains and lay scattered on the tracks. He also collected dry pieces of wood from the bushes growing along the track. These collections were carefully stowed into the cloth bag he carried.

His prized catch, the kite, its string securely grasped in his left hand, fluttered in the wind like a trapped bird trying to fly free.

"You know what I do with these?" he raised the bag containing coal and dry wood.

I raised my eyebrows, unsure.

"This is fuel for our cooking. I collect it for my mother."

Soon we reached a settlement called Seelampur.

Seelampur was not far from the railway track we were walking along. I had heard about this settlement from my father, who often recounted tales of the Partition to me. He had told me how Seelampur had been built to accommodate refugees from Pakistan in 1947, almost fifteen years ago. Located just outside our town of Tripuri, this settlement had offered a stepping stone for many refugees who initially lived there, started businesses and then moved out to bigger houses.

My father also told me how it had made many residents of this settlement into dreamers, waiting their turn to become rich. It seemed strange to be here now with Vasu.

Vasu pointed towards a small house on the fringe of the settlement. It was made of bricks, with a single room and a courtyard bound by mud walls. There was big neem tree in the courtyard. In one corner, under the tree, there was an open kitchen with an earthen stove. Alongside that lay some dry sticks and pieces of coal, similar to what Vasu had collected from the track.

Vasu then told me about his grievous loss. "I lost my father three years ago, when I was just eight years old. My father used to make surma, pack it in small plastic containers and sell it to the passengers in state buses. I took over his business soon after his death."

"This is where I live now, with my mother and grandmother."

"You know my grandmother is an enlightened one and is our spiritual guide."

"My mother…she is currently not at home, works in few houses in the town," he spoke with his eyes downcast.

Then he pointed to a spot under the tree with a parallel row of bricks and a space to light a fire between them.

"And this is where I make my surma," he spoke with a regained pride.

"Wait I will show you something," he said and promptly went inside. He came back holding an object wrapped in a sheet of cloth. He opened the layers and revealed a multicoloured stone. As I stared at it, Vasu said, "You know, this is a precious stone. My father gave it to me. This is the only wealth left from our past grandeur."

"Wow," I exclaimed, fully impressed.

He put that stone in my hand. It was as big as an almond with predominantly shining blue and green hues. As I turned it in my palm, I saw different colours play inside it like a rainbow. I was fascinated.

"I am waiting for my Raj Yoga to begin and then I will have this stone fixed right in the middle of my crown."

I had become very curious, and asked, "How do you protect this thing from the thieves?"

Vasu dragged me inside into the only room they lived in. There were two beds laid out along the walls, with an open space between. The walls were decorated with different coloured kites, surely looted by Vasu in the past. His last catch was yet to join them.

On one of the beds sat an old lady, his grandmother, fully covered with a thin white cotton sheet and humming religious hymns.

Vasu pointed towards a corner.

"You see these," he said. "These are Ravana's ribs. I collected these in the last two Dussehras. Do you know if you have even one of these, no thief will dare enter your house?"

There were two bamboo strips lying against the wall. Both were about two inches wide and four to six feet long and partially blackened, due to incomplete burning

Looking at my confused expression, he explained further, "You know when they burn Ravana's effigy on Dussehra day and before the whole thing turns into ash, you have to pull out one of his burning rib for yourself. That's what I did."

It was now clear to me what the source of those ribs was.

Then there was a sudden flutter and a white pigeon entered and sat on Vasu's shoulder. Apparently excited to see Vasu, the pigeon made giggling sounds with joyful nodding of his head.

"This is my pet called Moti." Vasu told me. There was apparently a special bonding between them and a proof of Vasu's connections with the birds.

All this ruckus disrupted Vasu's grandmother's meditation. She stopped her hymn singing and spoke from under her white cotton sheet. "Don't forget to get Ravana's third rib this Dussehra. That's what you need to attain your Raj Yoga."

"Yes, Dadi, I am anxiously waiting for that day," said Vasu, reassuring her.

"Also remember once you have the third rib you will no longer have to be Indrajeet."

I was again at a total loss about what was being discussed. Vasu helped me.

"You know, I play Meghnath, Ravana's younger brother, also called Indrajeet, in the Ram Leela that takes place every year."

"Because of my royal lineage, that role is below my dignity. However, once I have the third Ravana's rib and attain my Raj Yoga I will be straightaway promoted to play Lord Rama's role!"

"Believe me, they will not have any other choice then."

I returned home that day with my head fully stuffed with all that I had heard and seen. I told my parents only a few bits, which was enough for them to get alarmed. Worried about his unknown background, they forbade me to meet Vasu.

It was not to be like that at all.

Very next day I saw Vasu standing just outside our rear boundary wall.

There were two green parrots made out of aak fruit sitting on the wall and behind them was his smiling face.

I went close. Vasu had skilfully used different-sized green fruits of aak to make them look like parrots. Dry sticks were used to join them and to also make their legs. Black surma had been used to draw out the beak, wings and the eyes

"See, I made this parrot pair for you," he said.

Seeing me impressed he wanted to overwhelm me once again. "Come, I will show you today how we make the surma," he said.

Hypnotised, I followed him, holding aak parrots in my hands.

*

Once home, Vasu started the process of making surma. He filled two earthen lamps with oil and put cotton wicks in it; these had been soaked in sandalwood paste. He then lighted the lamps and placed them under the base of a bowl-shaped aluminium frying pan. There was some water in the pan to keep it cool. Slowly the soot created by burning wicks started to deposit on the pan's bottom.

Once enough soot had settled, he scraped some of it and put it in a small plastic container, which he then gave me as a gift. I was impressed again and Vasu knew that.

"This is a special surma," he said. "Nobody else uses sandalwood in their surma preparation."

"You know if I had a brass bowl rather than the aluminium one to collect the soot, the production would increase and the product would also be much finer."

"Do you have a brass bowl in your house you can spare?"

I thought of a brass container we had in our chicken pen, used to carry chicken feed.

Next morning Vasu was again standing outside our rear wall. I went on to our roof where our hens were kept, picked up the brass bowl and showed it to him.

His eyes brightened, "That will be excellent!" he exclaimed with excitement.

I threw it down to where Vasu stood, and he ran off with it.

Next day, I was curious and wanted to check whether my contribution had improved his surma production. I walked to his house. Vasu was nowhere to be seen. I looked around and could not spot the brass bowl either.

That evening my father enquired about that bowl, and I kept quiet. I came to know later that brass was a precious metal and could have fetched a reasonable sum if sold.

Days went by and I met Vasu less frequently. My parents were keeping an eye on me to stop our meetings. Perhaps they suspected Vasu to be behind the disappearance of the brass bowl.

Nevertheless, now and then he would suddenly appear outside our wall, every time with an aak green parrot.

*

It was monsoon season now and the Seelampur population was badly affected by rampant malaria.

One day, the maid who worked for us and came from that settlement told us that Vasu's mother has passed away after few days of fever. She knew that Vasu was my friend.

I got worried about Vasu and ran to his house. There were few people standing outside their home. I sneaked in. Vasu's mother's body, wrapped in a white cloth, lay on the ground. His grandmother was sitting motionless on the cot, under her thin white cotton sheet, as before.

Vasu was sitting near his mother's head. He looked at me; his piercing eyes showed signs of anger. He stood up and approached me. "Why have they tied up my mother in that white sheet?" The tears in his eyes had washed the dark surma down onto his cheeks.

"Where is her crown? Why is my mother lying on the floor? You have to respect a queen."

The people standing around looked at him. Nobody said anything; they just gave him looks of sympathy.

Confronted with a dead body wrapped in a white sheet made me feel sick. That was first time ever I had seen a dead person. I couldn't take it anymore and ran back to my house.

*

I didn't see Vasu for a few weeks. Then one morning I saw a pair of aak-fruit parrots sitting on my wall again. I couldn't see Vasu, though I knew he was there. I raised myself over the wall to look outside. He was sitting beside the wall looking at the ground. I jumped outside and hugged him.

He looked at me feverishly but didn't say a word. Then he dragged me to the peepal tree and as before climbed the rock.

"Just wait for this Dussehra. I am going to get the third rib," he spoke rather resolutely. It was more of a pledge.

"I have had enough of this world denying me my rightful place."

*

Not long after, the preparations for Ram Leela started. The following day, a procession of followers behind a decorated van went through our streets. The van had been made up to look like a chariot. The participating cast, wearing full make up, was there in the van. Vasu was also there, in the full getup of Meghnath and sitting in the rear of that van, facing backwards. It was obvious that his request to be given Lord Rama's role had been denied. I watched the van from my roof. Vasu sat motionless and looked at the ground as the van moved forward.

I made sure this time to go to all the Ram Leela shows with my father. One day, Vasu's turn came to appear on the stage. With a small crown on his head, wearing a colourful loincloth and holding a sword he stood on the stage and declared, "My name is Meghnath. Some people call me Indrajeet. I never, never, never accept defeat. Ha Ha Ha!"

Then he rushed down the stage, threw away his crown and sword and disappeared. He had seemingly emphasised "never, never" as if sending a clear message.

The next time I saw him was on Dussehra day, the tenth day of Vijaydashmi, when Ravana's effigy is burned, along with those of his two brothers, Meghnath and Kumbhkarana. This is to celebrate the victory of good over evil.

I went there with my parents. As we watched, Meghnath's effigy was first to be burned after being hit by an arrow by the man who played the role of Lakhsmana, Lord Rama's younger brother. As the fire consumed it, I thought of Vasu and wondered what he must be feeling watching Meghnath's effigy burn. I was sure he was there somewhere, for everyone would go to Dussehra fair in our town.

Next was Kumbhkarana's effigy's demise. Then came the finale everybody had been waiting for: it was time for Ravana to die. Standing almost twenty feet tall, the effigy was shot at with a fire arrow by Lord Rama. The arrow hit Ravana on his belly and he started to burn. The volunteers and police now started to push everybody back. They repeatedly announced that this year there were many more explosives and fireworks in that effigy.

Soon the flames which had started from the middle of his body, took over the whole structure of Ravana's effigy, reaching up towards his huge face and ten heads. The heat was unbearable. There was panic and a stampede among the spectators. Everybody ran back, away from the fire and fireworks. There were loud sounds of explosives and many colourful fireworks all around the burning effigy.

Suddenly a shadow emerged from among the crowds and rushed towards the burning effigy of Ravana. I knew it was Vasu. Nothing could thwart him that day. He rushed towards the base of that burning structure, even as many pieces of burning wood from the huge structure were raining down.

Thousands of people were screaming and pleading, asking him to come back, warning him about the danger he faced. He was determined. He had selected to jump straight into that delusional black hole his parent's death had created. His grandmother, his spiritual guide, had shown him the way into it.

For him it was now or never. He started to pull out a burning bamboo piece, trying to rip it from the burning structure. That pull was enough to shake the weakened and mostly burned structure and make it collapse.

Ravana's massive face and its ten big heads, engulfed in live flames, came crashing down and landed right on top of him.

I closed my eyes. Collective screams were raised everywhere, with loud cries of "Save him. Save him!"

A standby fire brigade went forward and succeeded in extinguishing the fire with great effort. They pulled the remains of the effigy away. Vasu's half-burnt body lay still on the ground, his right hand tightly clutching Ravana's third rib.

* * *

The Feast

The thick misty glass and the boiling water were no barriers to their agitated voices.

"He can't hear."

"He doesn't feel pain."

"Anyway he can't remember, his memory is very short-lived."

"Don't worry, even if he did, he won't talk," someone laughed.

"Eh, hurry up, raise the damn temperature, uh, add salt."

Their words hit my brain like spears.

Then somebody poked me. My body squirmed; I retracted, gathered my limbs for protection, hoping hopelessly to get away.

A conqueror's laugh hit my fragile brain again. I let go a voiceless cry, but they didn't hear.

In my futile attempt to stay alive, my failed hearing tried to catch their voices. My eyes were losing sight; theirs were lighting up. My arms collapsed, and theirs rose in rejoicing. It hurt to move my limbs while they merrily jumped with joy. Their mood and appetite soared. My cries created no ripples but their rejoicing shook the room.

Heat began extinguishing my senses. Then time slowed, as did the rising bubbles. My life seemed to have been prolonged; it was time's dying gift. The echoes of their baleful voices started to recede; leaving my head and the room behind. What remained was the grip of time.

The heat reached my soul and the bond between my body and my consciousness was slowly severed. Their feast was almost ready now.

Epitaph for a doomed lobster – *"Only 7 years old. Could have lived for long – if allowed!"*

Cooked Alive.
Luminous faces, blurred by heat,
The bubbling medium couldn't hide their greed.
As they grew hungrier for the anticipated meal,
Their voices got louder with animated zeal.
I lay in a corner, my eyes squealed,
I had no voice, I couldn't scream.
They smiled and said, "He can't feel pain",
I squirmed, retracted limbs, to get away in vain.
"He won't remember", another voice crowed,
I retracted my legs from his advancing probe.
Eyes open or closed – the vision unchanged,
Those words echoed in my head, again and again.
The breath I held stayed imprisoned,
Then the room became darker as did my vision.

* * *